THE
DEER
STAND

A. M. Monson

Lothrop, Lee & Shepard Books
New York

ACKNOWLEDGMENTS Special thanks to Pat Olson and Teresa Meillier for their willingness to share their time and knowledge, and also to Roger Grosslein, Pat Savage, David Spong, and the Hanson fellows.

First Edition 1 2 3 4 5 6 7 8 9 10

Library of Congress Cataloging in Publication Data
Monson, A. M. The deer stand / A.M. Monson.
p.   cm. Summary: When her family moves from Chicago to the wilds of Wisconsin and Bits has trouble making new friends at school, she spends her time trying to tame a deer in the woods near her house. ISBN 0-688-11057-6 [1. Deer—Fiction. 2. Friendship—Fiction. 3. Moving, Household—Fiction.] I. Title. PZ7.M7628De 1992 [Fic]—dc20 91-32122 CIP AC

FOR SUSAN
who gave me support and
opportunity,
AND FOR JACKIE
who always listened and
encouraged me to reach deeper.

1

With a thud, Bits dropped her black-and-coral backpack on the kitchen table and collapsed onto the couch. Her life was ruined. Today proved it.

Mom came down the hall carrying Jason. "So, how did school go?"

"Terrible!" answered Bits. "Worse than terrible."

"It can't be that bad," said Mom, setting Jason on the floor. She grabbed some nearby toys and placed them in his lap.

"Oh, yeah?" challenged Bits. "Mrs. Carlson refuses to call me Bits." She sat up straight and imitated her seventh-grade teacher. "I always address a student by his or her given name." Bits slumped against the couch. It wasn't *her* fault she hadn't been able to pronounce Elizabeth correctly until she was four. Up until then it always came out Lizbits. Why couldn't Mrs. Carlson be like her old teacher in Chicago and call her Bits?

"The kids treat me like I was an alien or something."

What a weird name, she'd overheard a couple of boys say. Then as if that weren't enough, she'd caught a couple of girls in her homeroom staring at her right ear. So she had three earrings—so what? She'd said hi to them, but they'd turned away and snickered.

"Nobody talked to me all day." Bits picked at the button on the couch pillow.

"It takes time," said Mom, closing the front window that faced the lake. "You're lucky to be in school. You're bound to make friends."

"I had friends back home," said Bits.

The window shut with a thud. "We all left friends behind, Bits. But we promised your dad to make the best of this move."

"That was before I knew we'd be moving into the wilderness."

"Northwestern Wisconsin is *not* the wilderness," snapped Mom.

Bits pulled the pillow to her chest. She'd done it again. It seemed like all she did lately was irritate Mom.

Mom took a deep breath. "Why don't you take a walk and see how pretty the September sunshine makes everything."

Jason started to cry, and Mom reached down to

pick him up. "Go on," she said, the anger gone from her voice.

Bits pushed the pillow away. As she dragged herself past the desk, she couldn't help but notice the fat, white envelope sitting on top. It was addressed to Anita, Mom's best friend in Chicago. Why didn't Mom just call her? She shrugged and grabbed an apple on her way out the door.

She didn't touch the wooden railing. Her forefinger was still sore from the splinter she'd gotten when they moved in on Friday. Looking around, she finally figured out what bugged her about living in the woods. It was too quiet! Except for a black-and-white bird pecking at the bird feeder, there wasn't a sound. Bits kicked a pinecone. It rolled over the ground and came to a stop next to a clump of dirt. She sighed, then started down the trail.

A canopy of pine boughs shaded her as she went deeper into the forest. The trees grew closer together, and there was little underbrush. She weaved and ducked her way around low, bare pine branches.

The soft, uneven green moss beneath her feet was dotted with animal droppings that reminded Bits of the rabbit turds she'd seen in the pet store. She stopped. How she longed to be with Celie, riding a city bus toward the mall.

First, they'd head into the shop that sold used

motorcycle jackets. They would look at earrings. Then they would go across to the pet store to watch the macaws. Most of the time the big, blue birds were so loud they had to plug their ears and hurry to the back of the store. There they played with the puppies. Always they left empty-handed. No pets were allowed in Celie's building, and Bits couldn't have any because both Mom and Jason were allergic to animal dander.

Bits felt the quiet creeping up on her. She grabbed a dead stick and bent it. Crack! Holding her arms out, she trotted down the trail, the ends of the sticks clattering against branches and tree trunks.

Finally she came to a T. To the left a path wound toward the lake. She'd explored it yesterday. Did the water ever warm up enough to go swimming? She doubted it, and even if it did, she wouldn't want to jump in. Bits imagined green slimy things touching her arms and legs. She shuddered, then turned to the right.

Soon she came across an iron pipe stuck in the ground with a faded orange ribbon tied to it. It was just like the one near their driveway that Dad said marked their property. One side was theirs, the other was owned by the paper company that now employed her father.

Past the pipe a fallen tree blocked the way. Bits crawled over it and continued on. The trail was

narrow for a hundred feet, then widened enough for a car. Newly cut stumps dotted the slight incline on the right. Up ahead good-sized evergreens with reddish bark lined both sides of the trail. Those must be the pines Dad said the paper company planted and harvested when they were mature. He called them Norway pines, but said most people up here called them red pines. Bits wondered how her Dad kept track of all the trees.

To the left of the pines was a clump of white tree trunks—and something else. Bits squinted to make out what the gray form was. She went closer to get a better look. It was a ladder! It rose twelve feet up the trunk of the white tree facing the clearing.

Bits touched the weather-beaten boards. Five steps led up to a small platform braced with a board tied to the top step and lashed with rope to the tree. She grabbed the rungs and climbed up. She had to turn around before she could sit down. Leaning against the tree wasn't comfortable, so she scooted closer to the edge.

Splashes of red and burnt orange dotted the landscape. A huge red pine stood by itself in the middle of the clearing, its boughs revealing glimpses of sky. Beyond the clearing the evergreens crowded together, reminding Bits of people jamming a busy store elevator just before the door closed.

Didn't Dad say there was a stream nearby that

emptied into the lake? Maybe on the other side of those trees. He said the paper company couldn't cut near the stream because it was a wildlife habitat.

Bits pulled the apple from her pocket and took a bite. She swung her feet back and forth between the ladder supports. This was a pretty spot, but why would someone build a ladder out here in the middle of the woods? She began to hum a song she heard on the radio that morning.

"Ba ba boom, ta da da . . ."

She and Celie could imitate all their favorite singers. Sometimes shy Shanti would join in. Even boy-crazy Kersten would stop thinking about boys long enough to sing with them. Bits swallowed hard. She looked at the apple in her hand, then flung it as far as she could. It landed on the other side of a fallen tree.

Dad was home in the garage collapsing moving boxes when Bits got back. "Just in time," he called. "Help me tie these. I want to drop them off at the recycling station tomorrow."

Bits took the ball of string from his outstretched hand. She wondered how people decided they didn't like living in the city anymore. Did it happen overnight or did it take weeks? When her dad first raised the subject of their moving, he said he missed the country. But why move now? Why not wait until she graduated from high school? Why uproot her four weeks into seventh grade?

Dad took a deep breath. "Do you smell it?"

"What?" She didn't smell anything.

"The pines. And I can even pick out some sweet fern."

"Sweet what?"

"Sweet fern. It looks like a fern, only smaller, and it won't curl up and turn brown until there's a hard frost. In the spring you'll really notice the smell." He smiled. "You know your great-uncle, Stan, used to live up here. He was a lumberjack. Sometimes I'd stay with him and Aunt Esther."

Bits finished tying a knot on a pile of flattened boxes. Here was Dad talking about some plant, and she was stuck out in the sticks. "I'm going to call Celie."

"Whoa, wait a minute." Dad straightened. "I'm not earning the money I did in the city, so I don't want you running up the phone bill calling Celie. Wait until Sunday, then you can call her."

"But Dad . . ."

"No buts. If you can't wait to tell her something, write a letter. I'll mail it in the morning on my way to work."

Bits groaned. Write a letter? What was this? The Stone Age? She stomped into the house. In her bedroom she found a notebook and started writing.

Dear Celie,
    I'm so bored up here, I think I'll die.

School's terrible. Mom says I'll have lots of chances to make friends at school. She hasn't been to *this* school.

Mom misses Chicago, too. I saw another envelope sitting on her desk. That's the second letter in four days.

I keep hoping Dad will change his mind about living up here and I'll wake up tomorrow and he'll say, "Hey, it's all been a mistake. Pack your bags, we're going back."

Wish I was there with you.

Love,

Bits

P.S. Do you think your mom and dad would like a third child? Just kidding. Write soon. Please!

2

The next morning Bits made sure the letter was sealed inside the envelope. She didn't want it accidentally falling out and getting lost. Quickly she slid it next to her dad's cereal bowl, then went to catch the school bus.

She cringed as the bus pulled up to her. Through the open windows she heard voices suddenly hush. Since she was the last one picked up there was only one seat left, the one behind the bus driver. The voices started whispering again, and every so often somebody laughed. Bits knew everybody was talking about her. She felt their stares boring into the back of her head.

Bits was out of her seat and on the steps before the bus came to a complete stop. She ran toward the school doors, imagining a trail of smoke coming from her hair. She dumped her things quickly into her locker, then hurried to homeroom, thankful her desk was against the back wall.

* * *

That afternoon when Mom asked how school had gone, Bits said okay and headed for her room. What was the point of complaining that no one talked to her again? Mom would only tell her it takes time to make new friends.

Bits dropped her backpack on the bed. There was tons of algebra homework. Mr. Fritch, the math teacher, had given her ten sheets of problems. "Do these as fast as you can. If you fall too far behind the whole year will be difficult." Bits hadn't been sure if he meant it would be difficult for her or for him.

There was also an assignment for Mrs. Carlson's English class, an essay on the most exciting thing that happened to you in the past week. Bits sighed. She thought about titling hers "The Ruination of Bits Patterson."

"Going for a walk," called Bits, closing the door behind her. She'd leave her homework until later. That way she wouldn't have time to think of all the things she could be doing back home.

She thought about exploring, but the ladder in the clearing intrigued her. She hauled herself up and sat down.

"So, how about it, red pine?" Bits held out an imaginary microphone. "Tell the audience why this ladder is out here." A pause. "No?" She turned to the trunk behind her. "How about you, birch tree?"

"I know!" Bits threw her arms wide. "This is a new world and I am queen of it all. Queen Bits of

Pinelavia!" she announced. "Start the fanfare! Sound the trumpets!" She brought a closed hand up to her mouth. "Tu-tu-tu-tu-duuuu. Te-te-te-deeee. Ta-ta-ta-dahhhh."

What was that? Bits dropped her imaginary trumpet. Did she see something? A branch moved in the trees thirty feet to her left.

"Oh, God," she whispered. "What if it's a bear or something?"

The branches parted. A head and two front legs poked through.

Bits blinked. The animal had antlers. "Wow! It's a deer."

Two dark brown eyes looked up at her.

"Hi."

The deer didn't move.

"Did you like my trumpeting?"

He tilted his head in her direction. Bits could see his black nostrils flare as he tested the air.

"I don't have B.O. if that's what you're sniffing for." He licked his nose with his tongue. Bits leaned forward to get a closer look. The deer whirled around. A white flash from his raised tail, and he vanished into the forest.

"Hey wait!"

Bits trumpeted, hoping he'd come back. After several minutes, her lips tired and she lowered her hand. Suddenly she scrambled down the ladder. The deer had come from over by the fallen tree.

Where was the apple she'd thrown there yesterday? She searched the ground, but didn't see it. Maybe he had eaten it.

Bits removed today's apple from her pocket, tossing it into the air a few times, then catching it. It was worth a try. She placed the apple carefully on the tree, then turned and raced for home. She couldn't wait to tell somebody about the deer.

Bits leaned against the garage entrance to catch her breath. Dad was home, collapsing cardboard moving boxes.

"Guess what I saw?" she panted.

He looked at her. "What?"

"A deer! In the woods near the stream. It had a black nose and small antlers." She stuck her index fingers in the air. "His antlers are like this, only longer, and curved." She bent her fingers slightly.

"Sounds like a spike horn," said Dad. "Bucks in their second year will have either spikes like you described, or if they have plenty of good food, they develop fork horns."

"Are those bigger?"

"Yes. Fork horns have an extra tine on each antler. My dad called them 'forkies.' He used to say spike horns and fork horns were the teenagers of the deer family." He crushed the box he was holding. "You were lucky to see him. Bucks are pretty good at staying out of sight."

Bits smiled. A teenager of another species. Well, since they were the same age, so to speak, it was meant for her to tame him, right?

Taking the steps two at a time, she burst into the house. She *had* to talk to Celie. So what if the first letter hadn't arrived yet? She wouldn't mind getting a letter two days in a row.

After dinner, Bits sat at her desk. She'd already finished the essay for Mrs. Carlson's class. She had written every detail she could remember about seeing the deer. Now she pulled out the algebra worksheets Mr. Fritch had given her. She groaned as she read the first question: "A girl will be y years old three years from now. Represent her age four years ago." She hated questions like these. After three of them she put her head on the desk.

The soft breeze outside carried a chorus of sounds up from the swamp. Must be a thousand frogs singing down there, thought Bits. She closed her notebook and shut off the light. Leaning against the window sill, Bits was surprised by how much she could see. The trail leading to the lake was bathed in a soft, white glow. Through the trees the water twinkled under the full moon.

Bits cocked her head. She heard a faint rustling sound in the woods to the right. It stopped, then started again. Could it be the deer, she wondered? Quickly she retrieved the flashlight from the hall

closet. The window above her bed faced in the direction of the sounds. Kneeling on the bed, she aimed the flashlight into the woods.

At first she didn't see anything except trees and branches, then she spotted something. Two yellow eyes stared back at her. Bits pulled back from the window. Then feeling foolish for being scared, she made herself lean forward again. Bits saw hundreds of quills covering the animal's body and tail. The porcupine lumbered out of the flashlight's range and disappeared.

Bits sank down on her bed. Moonlight shone on her bedroom wall. She still heard the porcupine moving about outside. Even the frogs belching in the swamp were louder than a few minutes ago. In the distance an owl hooted. Great, one more sound to keep me awake, thought Bits. She reached to close the window.

3

Two days later, six essays were posted on the bulletin board in Mrs. Carlson's homeroom. All six had big red A's in the upper left corners. Hers was the last one. Two boys were standing next to the board. The skinny one, Jeremy, sat in front of her; his friend's name was Travis. They'd been caught passing a note the day before.

"What a joke!" said Travis.

"Yeah," agreed Jeremy, "she gets an A for seeing a deer. Like it's the only deer around."

Travis brought his hands up to his head, stuck up two forefingers, and lifted his legs high as he walked.

Jeremy laughed and joined the act. "La la la," he sang in a high-pitched voice. "Oh, look! A deer!"

When they noticed her, the boys jostled each other and walked away laughing.

Bits felt her face and ears turn red. She strode to her desk and plopped down. Of course everyone up here had seen deer. How could she have been so

dumb? Now everyone was going to think she was weird. An idiot.

Bits studied the gray sky. How appropriate, even the weather matched her mood. She rotated her inch-long rhinestone earring between her thumb and forefinger. She wished a letter would arrive from Celie. It was too early, but that didn't stop her wishing.

The twelve o'clock bell sounded. Bits slowly closed the book on her desk. Lunchtime was the worst part of the day. On Monday she'd rushed to the lunchroom with everyone else, but no one else came to the empty table where she was seated. Since then, she waited as long as possible before getting in line.

The cafeteria tables were lined up in three rows of six, four chairs on each side of the table. Bits sat down facing the window. Now, rain pelted the glass panes. A girl with a floppy braid sat down across from her.

"Hi," said the girl.

Bits looked around. "You talking to me?"

"No, dummy, I'm talking to my pizza."

"It's just . . ." Bits decided not to tell the girl she was the first one to talk to her. She might think it was strange and leave.

"I hate tomatoes in food," continued the girl.

She peeled off the rubbery cheese, then scraped

the tomato sauce from the white, soggy crust, pushed the cheese back on the crust and took a bite.

"I can still taste the tomato sauce." She wrinkled her nose and let the slice drop back to her plate. Resting her elbows on the table, with her chin in her palms, she looked at Bits. "I like your earrings."

"Thanks," said Bits.

"The middle one is a dolphin, isn't it?"

Bits's fingers felt the second earring. "Yes," she answered. She'd had her hair cut short above the ear on that side, so that she could show off her earrings. The light brown hair on the left side of her head came to her chin.

"Where'd you get it?"

"At the Chicago Zoo gift shop. Our class went there on a field trip."

The girl sighed. "We never go anywhere."

The material covering the girl's left elbow was worn and a small hole showed her skin. Maybe her parents didn't have a lot of money, or perhaps she was just being cool. Suddenly the girl put her arms down and sat up straight.

"My name's Chris, Chris Howard. I'm in Fritch's homeroom."

"I'm Bits."

"I know," said Chris, tucking a loose strand of dark hair under her braid.

Bits stared at her.

"Word travels fast when someone new comes," explained Chris. "Most of us have gone to school together since kindergarten."

There was a scream at another table. Bits turned in time to see two girls from her homeroom jump up from their chairs. Pop dripped from the table onto the floor. Travis and Jeremy grinned at the girls from across the table.

"Just you wait, Travis!" growled one of the girls, wiping her skirt.

"I'm so-o scared," said Travis, shaking in mock fear. He and Jeremy strutted away, laughing.

Chris groaned. Bits turned back to her. "Who are those two?"

"The two boys?" asked Chris.

"No, the two girls. I know one is Karen." They were the same ones who laughed at her on Monday.

"The other girl is Julie. Her parents own the biggest resort in the area. Karen's dad is president of the bank."

Bits nodded. Well, at least she knew a little more about them now. That still didn't explain why they acted so snobbish, though. She hadn't done anything to them.

"I hang around with them sometimes," said Chris.

The bell rang. Bits whirled toward the clock. It *couldn't* be time already. They'd just start talking. When she turned back, Chris was already at the

dishwashing counter. Bits grabbed her tray and hurried to catch up.

"Bye," said Chris.

Still holding her tray, Bits watched Chris walk away. Had she made a friend? She bit her lip. If only Chris had said "see you" or "talk to you later," something other than good-bye. Bits didn't know if Chris wanted to talk to her again.

That afternoon when she came home from school, she grabbed two apples from the fruit crisper.

"Don't get filled up," called Mom from the other room. "I have a big dinner planned."

"Okay," answered Bits. She peeked into the living room. Mom was sitting at her desk, writing. Good, thought Bits. With Mom preoccupied she'd have more time to find other foods to feed Buck. What else? Back in Chicago, Kersten had told her that horses liked carrots. Bits opened the other crisper. Of course Kersten had let this information slip when she told Bits about the cute boy that lived near her uncle's horse farm. Smiling, Bits pulled a carrot out and stuck it in her pocket. Chair legs scraped against the floor in the living room. She closed the refrigerator door and ran outside.

Once on the damp trail, Bits smelled something. There were several single-stemmed plants about twelve inches high to her left. She plucked a couple of the fernlike leaves, and raised them to her nose.

They were sweet. She took another whiff. Was this the sweet fern her dad told her about? Wouldn't it be something if next spring the whole forest smelled like a perfume bottle! Bits groaned. She was starting to sound like her dad. She tossed the leaves aside and continued on her way.

She sat on the tiny platform waiting for the deer to show. At first she made trumpeting sounds, hoping his curiosity would bring him back again. But still the food sat on the fallen tree. She scanned the clearing, her eyes settling on the giant red pine.

"O Christmas tree, O Christmas tree." She giggled.

"With faithful leaves unchanging;
Not only green in summer's heat,
But also winter's snow and sleet,
O Christmas tree, O Christmas tree,
With faithful leaves unchanging."

She sang through three verses and was almost ready to give up when she heard a twig snap off to her left.

"O Christmas tree, O Christmas . . . "

The deer poked his head in the clearing.

"I'm glad you came back," said Bits softly. This time she didn't move a muscle. "I have a present for you."

His ears were erect and turned toward her. He smelled the air, lifting his nose toward the log.

"That's right, it's food. I hope you like apple and carrot."

It looked like someone had taken white eye shadow and smeared it above and below his eyes. He also had a white rim behind his black nose. It ran down to his mouth on both sides like a droopy mustache.

He watched her, his ears twitching toward any little sound.

"Nervous, aren't you?" said Bits.

He inched his way toward the fallen tree. He hesitated, then stretched his neck out and pulled the apple into his mouth.

"Sweet, isn't it?" said Bits. Chunks of white pulp fell from his lips as he chewed. "I can't eat too much sugar. I get cavities real easy." She looked at him with envy. "I suppose you never have to go to the dentist."

The deer raised his head and looked at her.

"Did you know the top of your nose looks like a horseshoe?"

The deer's head disappeared for a moment behind the fallen tree. When it reappeared a second later, he was chewing a piece of apple that he'd dropped.

"At the park Celie and I used to go to, there were these two really old guys who played horseshoes all the time. They let us try once. We couldn't throw as far as they could, so they let us stand closer to the

iron pipes. I got a ringer my first try. Celie was terrible—she barely hit the sand pit." She watched the deer clean up the remaining apple. "I sure wish you could talk."

The breeze rustled the few remaining birch leaves above her head.

"How about if I call you Buck?" said Bits. "That's what you are, and I think Bits and Buck sounds good, don't you?"

He stopped chewing. One ear twitched to the left. Bits didn't hear anything, but the deer dove into the brush and disappeared.

"Come back tomorrow," called Bits.

4

It was raining Friday morning as Bits walked down the driveway to catch the school bus. Large drops of water clung for a split second to the rim of her umbrella, then fell to the soft sand. Every drop made a tiny crater.

Inside the bus, she cleared the fogged-up window with her hand and looked outside. Would Chris have lunch with her again? How nice it'd be to talk to someone her own age. She had a thousand questions. What did Chris like to do on Friday nights? Did she have brothers and sisters? Who were her friends? Were there others besides Julie and Karen?

Walking down the hallway to her locker, Bits saw Julie and Karen coming from the opposite direction. They stared at her umbrella with its loon's head handle (it even had a red eye) and black and white striped material like a loon's body. She heard the two girls giggling as they passed.

Bits shoved the umbrella inside her locker. Mom

insisted she take it. Maybe she'd leave it at school, then Mom couldn't make her use it again.

"Where'd you get that weird umbrella?" asked Chris, walking up to her.

"It's my mom's," answered Bits. "Some nature store in Chicago was selling them." Funny how things that were popular in the city were considered strange up here.

"We get a lot of vacationers from Chicago during the summer," Chris leaned against the next locker. "It must be exciting to live in a big city."

"It is," agreed Bits. "There are always things to do. Friday nights we'd go to the roller rink. On weekends Celie and I'd go to the Lincolnshire Mall."

"You got to go to the mall?" asked Chris.

Bits nodded. This was making her homesick.

"I'm going to live in a big city someday," announced Chris. "And every night I'll eat out at a different restaurant. I'll go to plays. See the ballet."

The bell rang.

Chris sighed. "Gotta go. Fritch gets angry if we're late." She left for her homeroom.

Shoot! Bits slammed her locker door. She'd gotten so wrapped up in thinking about home, she forgot to ask Chris to sit together at lunch. Oh well, she'd save her a place anyway.

Bits sat facing the lunchroom door. It was ten after twelve before she saw Chris. Julie and Karen were ahead of her. They were just about through the

line when Karen pointed to Chris's tray. Julie grabbed her throat and pretended to gag. Chris quickly took a small bowl from her tray and set it back on the glass shelf.

Bits was pretty sure Chris was putting back the lime jello with cottage cheese. It was nice to know she wasn't the only one who liked the awful-looking salad.

The three of them walked past the table where Bits was sitting. Chris didn't look at her; she was busy trying to balance her tray and keep up with the other two girls. They sat at a table against the far wall.

Bits poked at her spaghetti. She wasn't hungry anymore. She dropped her fork onto the plastic plate. What had she expected anyway? Chris told her she was friends with Julie and Karen sometimes. It wasn't as if they were best friends or anything. Besides, they'd only talked to each other twice. That certainly wasn't enough time to become best friends.

Bits watched the three of them secretly. Julie caught her looking and gave her a smug, all-knowing look. Bits blushed and dropped her eyes. If only Chris hadn't been so eager to put that salad back. Bits sighed. She wondered if Chris would ever talk to her again.

Bits picked up the peanut-butter cookie from her tray and took a bite. Well, at least she had *one*

friend. Did Buck like sweets? She carefully wrapped the cookie in her napkin, then put it in her pocket.

Bits daydreamed about Buck the rest of the afternoon. After she'd tamed him, they'd explore the thousands of acres of paper company forest together. Each logging trail would be a new adventure. Who knew what the two of them might find?

Stories about the elusive young woodland girl and her handsome deer companion would spread. People'd see them leaping through the forest. "How can it be?" they'd ask. "Is that girl a forest spirit? Does she possess magical powers?" She'd have friends then! Bits smiled.

"Two apples?" Mom asked, peering over her shoulder. "Didn't you eat lunch at school?"

"Yes, I ate," answered Bits.

Mom didn't say anything, but gave her one of those "come on, tell me what's going on" looks.

"I'm just hungry, that's all," said Bits. "Lunch wasn't very good."

"Well, I suppose I'm lucky you're eating fruit instead of junk food."

Bits edged toward the door. She had to leave before she told another lie.

"Before you go," said Mom, "I want you to watch Jason tomorrow afternoon. I'm finally going to meet some people up here."

"What time?"

"I'm leaving at 1:30, probably be back around four. Your dad has to work tomorrow, so you'll be here by yourself." She looked at Bits. "You won't be scared to stay here alone, will you?"

Bits shook her head no.

"Good." Mom squeezed her arm and smiled. "I'm glad to see you're adjusting to living up here."

Bits shifted her feet. "Can I go?"

"Sure."

Bits hurried outside and ran down the trail. She wasn't ready to tell Mom about Buck. He was her special find: the only one she could tell everything to. She took a deep breath. From now on she'd be extra careful taking food from the refrigerator.

When Bits reached her spot, she checked around the fallen tree. Everything was gone. Great! Now if only he showed up while she was there.

Bits took the apples from her pockets. She'd thought to bring the little pocketknife she'd found at a rest stop when they drove up from Chicago, but then Mom had interrupted her. Cutting the apples into smaller pieces might keep Buck from dropping the fruit as he chewed. Oh well, she'd get it tonight.

Bits backed up two steps nearer the birch trees and set the apples on the ground. Too bad she hadn't gotten a carrot, but Mom would have asked too many questions. She still had the cookie from lunch, though. Bits laid it next to the apples, turned, then crossed the twenty-five feet to the ladder.

She leaned her back against the side support, looked up and caught a glimpse of black and white. A dull knocking sound startled her. Then through the partially bare branches, she saw the woodpecker hitting its beak against the tree. Was it a hairy or downy woodpecker? She wasn't sure.

She knew it was a woodpecker because Mom was forever pointing out the different birds that stopped at their bird feeder. "See the wing bars and tail? Notice the beak and markings around the eyes." Bits wondered if Mom had described hospital patients the same way she described birds. Mom had worked on the oncology ward at a nearby hospital until three months before Jason was born. Bits had called it the "tumor hotel."

She heard the familiar sound of a car's engine backfiring in the distance. There was a gas station every few blocks in Chicago. But up here, anyone having car trouble would have a long walk to reach a phone, let alone a gas station.

Fifteen minutes and still no sign of Buck. Maybe Dad was right—she'd just been lucky to see him. "No," she said out loud. "He'll show up." She looked at the red pine in the clearing.

"O Christmas tree, O reddish tree,
Your boughs are huge and far apart."

Buck would show up.

"I wish my deer, he would get here,
My fingers are all frozen;
Oh, Buck, my deer, my song you'll hear
And meet me by the big red tree."

Bits shivered. The temperature had slowly dropped through the week and her windbreaker was no longer warm enough. Bits rubbed her arms. She'd wear her down jacket from now on. She couldn't wait any longer. Bits took one last look around. The clearing was quiet except for the song of a chickadee in the distance. There was no sign of Buck. How could she tame him, if he didn't show up when she was there? Her shoulders hunched, Bits trudged home.

5

The next afternoon, Bits paced the living room. Jason sat in his playpen, his hands clenched around pull-a-part toys. Bits stopped and glared at the big clock over the fireplace. It was twenty-eight minutes after four.

"Come on," she groaned, then went back to her pacing. Buck had come around this time.

Was that Mom's car? She ran to the door and yanked it open. A light wind moved the smaller boughs at the top of the jack pines. A red squirrel with a pinecone in his paws sat on the woodpile and scolded her for interrupting him.

"N-n-n-n, yourself," said Bits, slamming the door shut.

Her jacket lay on the table. In its pockets were one apple, two carrots, the little jackknife, and a bag of cornflakes. She'd remembered that Kersten had said her uncle planted a cornfield just for the deer. Bits didn't have any corn. Cornflakes were the closest she could come.

It was almost 4:30! Bits looked out the kitchen window and saw the glow of headlights coming down the driveway. She ran to the table and grabbed her jacket. Mom pulled into the parking spot just as Bits opened the door.

"Oh, good," said her mother, getting out of the car. "Help me carry in groceries and put them away."

"Groceries? Aw, Mom! I was going for a walk."

"You can go for a walk tomorrow. Now get over here and help me."

Bits knew by the tone of Mom's voice that there was no use arguing. "How come you're so late? You said you'd be home by four," complained Bits when she reached the car.

"Bits, this is the first chance I've had to make friends up here. I was talking and the time flew, then I had to stop and get groceries." Mom put her hand on Bit's shoulders. "I don't have the advantage of being in school like you."

Bits's eyes widened. Advantage!

"Here," said Mom, reaching into the car, then handing her a bag. "There are enough apples in there to last you at least a week."

Bits carried it into the house. On her last trip from the car two ravens flew through the twilight sky. Their calls reminded Bits of small children taunting her. "A-w-k you missed your deer, a-w-k you missed your deer."

Bits looked up at the sky, her jaw set. "Nothing will keep me away tomorrow. You hear that?" The ravens didn't answer.

"You know what I miss about the city?" asked Dad, when Bits came into the kitchen the next morning.

Bits felt her hopes rise. "What?"

"Having the Sunday paper delivered," he answered. "Up here you have to get dressed and drive twenty miles to get one."

"I miss Celie," said Bits, "and Shanti and Kersten, but mostly Celie."

"I suppose you have a whole list of things to tell Celie."

Bits straightened. A list wasn't a bad idea, then she wouldn't forget anything. "Yeah, I'm going to tell her about . . . "

"Yes?"

"Things."

"Private, huh?"

"Sort of." Bits squirmed under his gaze.

"Made any friends up here?"

"I thought I had," answered Bits. "A girl named Chris ate lunch with me on Thursday. And talked to me again Friday morning, but then when lunch came she went to sit with her friends."

"Maybe she's waiting for you to make the next move," said Dad, scratching his beard.

"Maybe," said Bits. She hadn't thought of that.

"You know if you want to invite anybody to come over for dinner or stay overnight, that's fine with us."

Bits nodded. It might be a while before that happened, but in the meantime she could talk to Celie. She bolted her cereal and dashed to the phone.

"I think you'd better wait until at least ten o'clock," said Dad. "You wouldn't want to wake them."

That was two hours! At least she had something to do. In her bedroom, Bits pulled out a sheet of paper and wrote down things she wanted to tell Celie:

Did she get my letter?
Does Celie know anything about deer?
Tell Celie I'm taming Buck.
Tell her about Chris and Julie and Karen.

She'd run out of things to put on the list, and it was only 8:15! If she concentrated on something else, maybe the time would go by faster. In desperation Bits pulled out her algebra worksheets.

At exactly one minute to ten, Bits carried the phone into her bedroom and dialed Celie's number.

"Hello?" Celie's sister, Tonya, answered the phone.

"Is Celie there?" She should be. Bits knew they didn't have church until eleven.

"Yeah, hang on."

Bits heard the phone drop. Several seconds passed. "Come on."

Finally Celie picked up the phone. "Hello?"

Bits could tell her friend was out of breath. "Hi, it's me."

"Bits!"

"Did you get my letters?"

"I've gotten one," answered Celie. "How many did you send?"

"Two."

"It'll probably come tomorrow," said Celie.

"I'm taming a deer," said Bits.

"You are?"

"He's beautiful. You have to come up and see him. On Friday—"

"Who is it?" A voice whispered in the background.

"Bits," whispered Celie.

"Hi, Bits." Shanti's voice came over the line.

"Hi," said Bits.

Celie came back on. "Shanti stayed overnight with me. She's going to church with us this morning."

Bits felt a twinge of jealousy creep over her. If she were home, she would be going with Celie instead of Shanti.

"So how are you? Is there anything to do up there?" asked Celie.

"Okay. There's not much up here," answered Bits. "Just a lot of trees and of course Buck."

"Who?"

"My deer."

"Oh," said Celie.

"Kersten, Shanti, and I went to the roller garden Friday night," said Celie. "It wasn't very busy, and we learned a line dance from some other kids."

"Sounds great," said Bits, trying to keep the quiver out of her voice.

"Look, Bits, I can't talk now," said Celie. "We have to get ready."

"I miss you," blurted Bits.

"We miss you, too," said Celie. "Gotta go. I'll write, I promise. Bye."

"Bye," said Bits, but Celie had already hung up.

Bits put the phone down. A tear rolled down her cheek. She wasn't going to cry. She just wasn't. She crumpled up the list and tossed it into the garbage can. Wiping away another tear, she carried the phone into the living room and set it on the small table next to the kitchen.

"You didn't talk long," said Dad. "Wasn't Celie home?"

"Yeah," answered Bits, "but she had company and couldn't talk."

"Oh." He came up and put an arm around her shoulders. "You can call her again later if you feel like it."

Bits nodded.

"How about coming outside and helping me with that firewood we had delivered last week. I'll split, and you stack."

"Okay," said Bits. She pulled on her jacket and followed him.

A pile of logs waited to be split on the other side of the garage. Dad set a long one on end, picked up the ax, swung and missed by a couple of inches.

"Did you see that?"

"What?"

"It moved."

"Huh?"

"The log," said Dad. "As soon as I swung, it moved just like that!"

Bits groaned.

Her dad smiled. "Had you going there for a second, didn't I?"

Bits shook her head. A slight smile tugged at the corners of her mouth.

"I'll get the hang of this, don't worry." He picked up the ax again.

While Dad took some practice swings, Bits wandered around the area behind the garage.

"What's this?" Several layers of gray, splintery boards were neatly stacked.

"They're from an old outhouse," answered Dad. "See the board on top, the one with the half moon cut into it?"

Bits fingered the hole.

"That was to let a little light in when you were doing you know what."

Bits imagined herself tiptoeing out into the darkness. Would she take a light with her, a candle perhaps? What if it went out? It would be scary sitting there in the dark, listening to all the sounds in the woods. She was glad they had indoor plumbing.

"Time to stack," called Dad.

It was a little after one when they returned to the house. Bits's hands were dirty from the eight-foot long, two-foot high row of split logs she'd stacked against the garage.

After lunch, she checked the time. It was almost two o'clock. Still a little early to go see Buck, but that was all right. It'd be better to get out of the house before Mom asked her to watch Jason or do the dishes. She pulled an apple out of the crisper and turned to see Mom staring at her.

"You just finished eating your lunch and a dessert," said Mom. "This craving for apples has me worried. You went through a five-pound bag last week." She looked at Bits closely. "I'm beginning to think there's a vitamin you're not getting enough of."

"Oh, Mom." Bits turned away. "I'm fine." Her mother's concern made her feel guilty. "This is for later, in case I get the munchies." She tried to act

calm, but sweat was beginning to drip down her sides.

"She looks good to me," said Dad. "She's even gotten some color in her face since we moved up here."

Mom sighed. "I suppose you're right, but still . . ."

Bits took this as her cue to escape and grabbed her jacket. "Be back later," she called, as the door shut behind her.

Whew! That was too close, she thought. She'd have to think of some other way to feed Buck. What if Mom realized the carrots were disappearing, too? How was she going to get more food? There wasn't a convenience store two blocks away like in Chicago.

Bits was still trying to come up with a way to get food when she came to the iron pipe. There was a noise off to her left. It sounded like branches crashing against one another. But how could that be? There was only a light breeze.

Bits strained to see, but there was too much brush. She climbed an incline off the trail to the right to get a better view. In the swampy ground near the stream, the tops of two young river birch shook violently. Their few remaining yellow leaves drifted to the ground.

She scrambled down the hill, ducking and weaving her way through the brush toward the young

trees. Suddenly, the sounds stopped. Bits sucked in her breath. What if it was an animal? What if it was now looking for her? Bits paused, her eyes searching the brush around her. The thrashing resumed. Bits continued cautiously toward the trees. Her foot sank into soft muck and dark brown water oozed into her tennis shoe. The dense brush snagged her hair and jacket. One more step, yes, now she could see something. It was a deer. Buck? She couldn't see enough of him to tell. Up and down his antlers raked the young saplings. Sections of bark were stripped, the bare wood exposed.

One more step and she might be able to tell. She scrambled onto an old fallen tree. It crumbled under her weight and she grabbed a branch to keep her balance. The brittle wood cracked under her hand.

The deer jerked its head up and whirled around. It *was* Buck.

"It's just me," said Bits.

Buck's nostrils flared. He stomped the ground with his front right hoof, then snorted.

"Sorry," said Bits. "Didn't mean to scare you." He was irritated with her for sneaking up on him. She must've interrupted something important, like the time she walked in on Mom and Dad kissing.

"I've got an apple for you," she said. Ever so slowly she reached into her pocket and pulled out the red fruit. She cut it into quarters and held one

out, so he would catch the scent before she threw it. She didn't want to scare him just when he was getting used to her.

Buck switched his tail once, then he dropped his head slightly. The wild look in his eyes softened a little. She tossed an apple quarter through the brush that separated them. He sprang into the air, landing six feet from the fruit. Bits winced. Why didn't he smell the apple? Bits felt her hair ruffle against her left cheek. Of course. She was downwind from Buck. No wonder she'd been able to sneak up on him. He couldn't smell her, and with all that noise he was making he hadn't heard her either.

The deer bobbed his head up and down. Now he smells the apple, thought Bits. Stiff-legged, he approached the fruit. It seemed to take forever. Finally he lowered his head and ate the treat. Bits threw the second piece two feet short of the first. Buck hesitated a moment, then took a step toward it.

With his head lowered, Bits could see the creamy white tips of his spikes. Near his head they turned a light gray. At the base of each antler brownish hairs stuck out as if they had been pushed out of the way by the antlers.

"You know you're the only one I can count on." Bits spoke softly. "I know Celie doesn't miss me as much as I miss her. She has Shanti and Kersten around." She was silent. "I'm not sure if I should keep writing letters to her."

Buck lifted his head, and she threw the next quarter.

"Chris, I don't know about her. She told me that sometimes she's friends with Julie and Karen. What does 'sometimes' mean? Does it mean we'll only be friends when she's not hanging around with them?" Bits frowned.

Buck jerked his head up. She must have spoken louder then she'd intended.

"It's okay," soothed Bits. "I didn't mean to scare you." She tossed the fourth piece to him. "I don't want to lose you, too."

6

Monday morning on the bus, Bits watched for Nelson's grocery store. It was on the right-hand side as you drove into town, a long, one-story building with a glass front. Nelson's sold a variety of things: furniture, appliances, and groceries. She'd even seen a few clothes hanging in the window.

The bus slowed and turned left off the highway onto Main Street. Nelson's was on the corner, across from the Helping Hand hardware store. On the next block the Trapper Bar had a red and white closed sign stuck in the window. Then came the Totogatic post office, followed by the Bank of Totogatic. Bits had never seen such a small bank. They passed through blocks of houses, then the Catholic church with the graveyard next to it. After one more block of houses the bus pulled into the school parking lot. Bits had counted eight blocks from the grocery store to school.

She'd have to go during lunchtime, which only gave her a half hour. Would anyone notice if she

disappeared? Probably not. There was one advantage to being new to the area.

Julie, Karen, and Chris were talking together near the stairway when Bits opened the school door. Bits didn't know what to do. She wanted to talk to Chris, but not when Julie and Karen were around. If she didn't talk to Chris soon, Chris might think she didn't want to be friends. She hurried past them to her locker. Things had never been this complicated in Chicago.

As she emptied her backpack, Bits studied the three girls. If only those two snobs would leave! Bits glanced at the clock. The bell would ring any minute. Bits banged her locker shut and marched over to Chris. It was now or never.

"Hi," she said.

Chris stuffed her hands into her back pockets and looked at the floor.

Julie and Karen glanced at each other. "We'll see you later," said Julie to Chris. They turned and sauntered away.

Bits wanted to yell "jerks," but didn't.

Chris remained silent.

"Maybe we can sit together at lunch tomorrow," suggested Bits.

"I—I can't," said Chris. "I'm sitting with Julie and Karen."

"Oh," said Bits. Should she try again? "How about Wednesday?"

Chris shook her head no. Bits got the picture. Chris didn't want to be friends, not even sometimes. She felt like a fool for even asking.

"Gotta get something out of my locker," she said quickly, and fled before Chris could see her eyes watering.

Bits opened her locker and pretended to look for something, then slammed the door shut. Well, Chris didn't want to be friends. Fine. She already had a friend. She had Buck.

The rest of the morning, Bits concentrated on what foods to buy her deer. There wouldn't be a lot of time once she reached the store. Besides, she only had five dollars and twenty-six cents. Carrots and apples were the first things on her list because she knew he'd eat those. She had gone back to the clearing after seeing Buck in the swamp yesterday and put down the carrot and cornflakes. When she'd stopped by the clearing this morning the carrot was gone but not the cornflakes. Deer must only like real corn. Would they have corn on the cob in the store? She'd have to check.

Bits counted down the seconds to lunch. At last, the fourth period bell rang and she hurried into the hall and dumped her books into her locker. She wanted to bolt out the door, but that might attract too much attention. Casually she walked out the front door, pretending she was one of the town kids

who went home for lunch. Once she was out of sight of the school, she broke into a run.

The bank and post office were open now, and the Trapper Bar door was ajar. A smell of stale beer and french fries wafted out, and Bits was suddenly hungry. She hadn't thought about food for herself. Oh, well, she could always eat an apple or a carrot once she got back to school.

Bits was panting when she reached the highway. Her side ached. She waited for a semi to pass and crossed the road to the store.

There were only two cash registers near the door. Bits was used to seeing a whole string of checkout lanes. This reminded her of Morrie's, the small market near their house in Chicago.

The produce section was at the back of the store. Quickly she grabbed a bag of carrots and a bag of apples. Next, she chose a head of lettuce, but put it back. Where would she keep it? Not in the refrigerator—Mom would ask too many questions. What else should she get? Bits picked up a pear. Would he like it? She could always come back for more. There wasn't any corn on the cob.

Near the bananas was a doorway leading into another room. Bits peeked inside. A row of handwritten signs advertised birdseed prices. Below the signs were large garbage cans full of sunflower seeds, thistle seed, and a mix of seeds with cracked corn.

Corn? Bits peeked inside the metal can. This wouldn't do. The corn was ground so small she could hardly tell it from the rest of the seeds.

Further down the aisle to her right, several white blocks were stacked on top of one another. The sign above read DEER SALT LICKS. Bits ran her finger across the lick's smooth surface, then touched her tongue. Whew, that was salty. At last, next to the blocks were fifty-pound bags of feed corn. Wasn't there something smaller? Across from the bags there was another garbage can half full of loose, yellow kernels. A roll of gallon-sized plastic bags hung nearby. Bits filled one with the corn.

It was seventeen minutes after twelve when Bits reached the checkout. She raced out the door—the food stuffed in her backpack. By the fourth block her lungs burned. Her legs grew wobbly between the sixth and seventh. She gasped for air as she climbed the school steps and had to use both hands to open the door. The fifth period bell was still ringing. She was safe.

In her bedroom that afternoon, Bits dumped the food on the bed. How much should she take? One apple and one carrot for sure. She poured the corn from the gallon-sized bag into the small plastic bag that had held cornflakes. The pear had squishy brown spots from banging into things: better take that, too. Bits filled her jacket pockets and inspected

herself in the mirror. Good, there weren't any bulges.

"I'm going outside," called Bits. She grabbed an apple. Mom entered the kitchen just as Bits reached for the door. She saw Mom look at the apple in her hand. "Nothing good for lunch," she said, slipping outside. This apple really was for her. She hadn't been able to eat anything until she scarfed down a carrot on the bus ride home.

Only the apple core remained by the time she reached the ladder. The week before she had laid the food on the ground a few feet behind the fallen tree. Bits decided to move the food closer to the ladder.

She broke the carrot in half, then put apple slices next to it on the rotten tree trunk. Stepping back toward the ladder a few feet, she poured the corn into a pile and circled the yellow kernels with pear slices.

What did that cooking teacher on television always say? The woman with the wobbly voice. Her mom watched the show all the time. *Bon appétit!* That was it.

She still had the two cores—one apple and one pear. "I wonder," she murmured, looking at the ladder and the birch tree trunk behind it. Reaching up as high as she could, she rubbed the cores against the white bark. Buck was always sniffing. Maybe the wind would carry the scent of food to him. It would signal him that she was here waiting. The fruit disin-

tegrated in her hands. She cleaned her sticky palms on the bark, removing as much of the pulp as she could.

Bits sat down and leaned against the ladder. The late September sunshine felt warm on her face. She shut her eyes. A raven cawed in the distance. Nearby another bird sang. "Chick-a-dee-dee-dee." Off to her right a red squirrel chattered.

Her eyes snapped open. Buck stood near the fallen tree. "I didn't even hear you come." She smiled. "I suppose that makes us even."

He stretched his neck toward the food.

"That's right," said Bits. "Eat that first, then you can show me how brave you are."

He quickly cleaned off the top of the tree, then hesitated, watching her.

"There's more," said Bits.

The deer didn't move. Bits wondered if she had made a mistake—moving the food too close too soon.

Buck took one step, then another. He rounded the fallen tree and stopped a couple of feet from the second food pile. His large brown eyes were glued to Bits.

"It's okay," Bits reassured him. She didn't know what else to do.

He lowered his head slowly to the food and jerked it back up a split second later to stare at her again.

Bits's eyes widened. What was going on? She stared back. It was the right thing to do. Buck relaxed, then dropped his head to eat. Bits smiled. He had been testing her, making sure she wouldn't pull something when he least expected it.

"You can trust me," she said softly. "Honest." She watched his lower jaw go around in circles as he chewed. The long white hairs in the middle of his ears stood out against the dark fuzzy rim. She knew his ears would be soft and she wanted to reach out and touch them.

"It's you and me," she whispered. "We'll be best friends."

She watched, entranced, as he finished the rest of the food.

7

Bits went to the clearing almost every day for the next two weeks. Sometimes Buck came, sometimes he didn't. But each time Bits moved the food closer to where she sat.

The last few days, Buck had come three times out of four. He'd even lifted his hind leg to scratch behind his ear with his hoof. Bits took this as a sign that he was getting used to her. Once she'd caught him yawning.

It was Thursday morning. The sun was peeking through the trees as Bits stood at the end of the driveway waiting for her bus. Slanted beams of soft light encircled her and played tag across the forest floor.

Bits was happy. Yesterday's storm was over. She'd barely had time to put out Buck's food before sheets of icy rain had pounded the ground. The wind had toppled a jack pine near the house. Bits was surprised more jack pines hadn't fallen over. It

had been a strong wind. Not only had the branches moved, the trunks had swayed back and forth like pendulums in grandfather clocks.

Bits peered down the road. There was no sign of the bus, but a faint flickering next to her attracted her attention. A spider's intricate web was stretched between two scrub oak branches. Tiny diamonds of water hung from the delicate strands. She reached out to touch one of the jewels.

Just then, the school bus roared around the corner. Bits jerked her finger away and severed four of the strands. She wiped her hand on her jeans, dismayed that she had destroyed such perfect symmetry.

She was standing in front of her locker pulling a notebook out of her backpack when Chris came up to her.

"Hi."

Bits looked up. "Oh, it's you." She put her pack down. "Where are your friends?" She put the emphasis on the word "friends."

"Who knows?"

Bits spotted them down the hall. Julie and Karen had their backs turned and were walking away. "You'd better hurry; they're leaving you behind."

"I don't care," said Chris.

Bits eyed her warily. "Why?"

"Because I like *you*."

You haven't for two weeks, Bits wanted to say,

but decided against it. "Julie and Karen won't like it."

"So what," said Chris, shrugging her shoulders. "They can find someone else to be their gopher."

"Gopher?"

"Yeah," said Chris. "Go for this, go for that. Get me a Coke. Do this algebra problem." She crossed her arms over her chest. "Look, do you want to be friends or not?"

Bits stared at her. Wasn't that her line? When she didn't answer, Chris turned to leave. "Wait!" Bits rubbed her forehead. She supposed she could give Chris another chance. "You want to sit together at lunch?"

Chris dropped her arms and smiled. "You bet." The bell rang. "See you later."

Bits watched Chris's loose braid swing from side to side as she walked away.

Bits thought about Chris all morning. Did she really want to be friends? It would be nice to talk to someone her own age, someone who could talk back. Buck wouldn't take offense. They were friends in a different way.

Establishing a friendship up here would probably take longer than in the city. Chris rode a different bus than Bits; they couldn't walk home with each other like she and Celie had done.

Celie. Bits wondered if she'd ever get a letter from

her. She pushed the thought quickly out of her mind.

Maybe Chris'd ask her home sometime. They'd go to Chris's room and talk. That is if she didn't share a room with a sister. If she did, Bits hoped it was a younger sister and not an older one. Younger sisters you could boss around.

The noon bell buzzed and Bits hurried to get into the lunch line. At first she didn't see Chris. Then she spotted her sitting at a table near the window.

"Do you have any brothers and sisters?" she asked, sitting down.

"A younger sister, Lisa, and two older brothers. Larry's a sophomore on the football team. He never has to baby-sit." Chris held out her arms like a linebacker and lowered her voice. "Got practice after school."

Bits laughed at her jock imitation.

"Then there's Jeremy."

"He's your brother?" asked Bits. She'd disliked Jeremy and his friend, Travis, ever since they'd teased her about her story on Buck.

"He's only a jerk when Travis is around."

"You don't look like twins."

"We're not," said Chris. "He's a year older."

Bits was relieved. "But you're in the same grade?"

"They held him back in second grade because he was sick. He missed too many days." Chris took a bite of noodle casserole. "How about you?"

"I have a younger brother."

"You're lucky," said Chris. "Ever wish you had an older sister?"

Bits thought about Tonya, Celie's sister. Older sisters were okay, she guessed, as long as they didn't get crazy when you touched something of theirs.

"I do," said Chris. "Then I could wear her old clothes instead of my bro—" Her cheeks grew red. "I—I see you get on the G bus. How far from Nancy Lake do you live?"

"I think we're on the northwest corner."

"Really? We're about a mile from the south end."

"Then how come we're on different buses?"

"They head in opposite directions. The G bus goes north from the lake; the H heads south."

The bell rang. Bits couldn't believe it. Every time she got into a conversation, the obnoxious bell was there, cutting it short. She'd be glad when Chris and she got some time away from school and could talk as long as they wanted to.

Bits had a hard time concentrating in her afternoon classes and Mr. Fritch noticed. He strolled down the aisle and stood next to her desk. Bits hadn't even copied any of the problems on the board yet. She scribbled them quickly on a piece of paper, and Mr. Fritch returned to the front of the room.

Bits's mind wandered back to her conversation with Chris. She couldn't believe it! She had a friend!

Of course, Buck was her friend, too. The first friend she'd made up here. Should she tell Chris about him? It might be better to show Buck to her. But she'd wait a while to make sure they were going to stay friends first.

"Elizabeth," said Mr. Fritch as Bits headed for the door, "I want to talk to you for a minute."

Bits could feel her classmates' "you're in for it now" looks burning into her back as they left the classroom.

"We're running out of time for you to finish those sheets I gave you." He took off his glasses and set them on his desk.

Bits didn't think he looked like a math teacher. He had thick wavy hair and a muscular build, and he was the assistant coach for the high-school football team.

"You need to catch up in the next week, or I'm afraid you'll be lost for the rest of the year. Do you think you can do that?"

Bits didn't know if she could get through it all.

"Perhaps you could stay after school, and I could help you in any areas you're having trouble."

"No!"

Right away Bits wished she could take the word back. She hadn't meant to say it that loud. "I mean—my mom will help me. She used to be a nurse and she knows all this stuff."

Mr. Fritch nodded. "Good. Then you'll be able to finish those sheets and catch up."

Bits looked at the clock. "Can I go?" As it was she was going to be walking into her science class five minutes late.

Mr. Fritch nodded, and Bits hurried out of the room. Boy, was that close. If she'd ended up staying after school, Mom would find out how far behind she was, and she could forget about seeing Buck. Mom would keep her chained to the table until she was sure that Bits understood every last problem.

Mom was on the phone when Bits got home that afternoon. She overheard her mention Saturday and hoped that didn't mean she'd have to baby-sit all afternoon again. Come to think of it, she hadn't seen Mom writing as many letters lately. These phone calls to people in the Save the Rivers group probably had something to do with that.

Bits hurried to her room and stuffed Buck's treats into her pockets, but Mom was waiting for her in the kitchen.

"I want to talk to you for a minute," she said firmly.

Bits panicked. Was the food showing? Had Fritch called?

"Sit down," said Mom.

Bits slid into a chair and waited for the ax to fall.

"Are you making any friends at school?"

"Huh?"

"Are you making any friends at school?"

"Well, yeah." So that's what this was about.
"Who?"

"Chris. She and her brother Jeremy live a mile from the other end of the lake."

"Anyone else?"

What did Mom expect? Was she supposed to make friends with the entire school in two weeks? "Jeremy's friend, Travis. He's talked to me. And Julie and Karen."

"Good." Her mother smiled. "I was getting worried. You never mention anyone, and all your walks alone. . . . " Her voice trailed off. "I just wanted to make sure things were going all right."

What would Mom say if she knew her daughter's closest friend had four legs and antlers? Bits wondered and smiled. She stood up. It was getting late. "Can I go?"

"Sure," answered Mom. "Invite Chris and Jeremy over sometime. Julie and Karen, too, if you want."

"I will," said Bits. She'd promise anything to get out of the house.

Bits tore out the door and down the trail, hoping Mom's little talk hadn't cost her today's visit with Buck.

8

That Sunday Buck ate at her feet. He'd even nuzzled her sneakers looking for more. Today she was sure he would eat out of her hand! Bits was so excited at the prospect of finally getting to pet Buck, she had to force herself to slow down as she raced to the clearing. She didn't want her pounding footsteps and panting to scare him.

She cut an apple in half and mashed the pulp against the birch bark. Then she emptied a bag of corn at the base of the ladder and placed the carrot halves on top of the yellow kernels. She pulled out a second apple and cut it into thirds. Finally she settled herself on the ladder, resting her wrists on her drawn-up knees. She held a piece of apple in her right palm, and the two other pieces in her left.

"I'm all set," she said aloud. If only she could snap her fingers and have Buck come running. Be patient, she told herself. It would take a few minutes for the fruit scent to reach him.

The boughs of the red pine were still against the blue sky. Had the sky ever been this blue in the city? Bits didn't think so—there was too much smog. She wanted to reach up and cut out a piece of it with her jackknife, then save it in a jar like other people saved rocks or sand from the ocean.

A lone yellow birch leaf fluttered briefly above her head, then stopped. Even the chattering red squirrels were quiet. Everything was perfect for coaxing Buck to eat out of her hand.

She didn't hear him enter the clearing, but she saw his slate gray coat out of the corner of her eye. "There you are," she whispered as he wound his way toward her. He paused. His mouth opened wide.

"Did you just wake up from a nap?" He looked sweet, like Jason when he was sleepy.

He continued toward her, but stopped again six feet away. His left ear flicked toward a sound she couldn't hear. He sniffed the ground. When he didn't find food, he cocked his head at her.

Was that a puzzled expression on his face, or was she imagining it? "I moved the food because I want to touch you," she explained.

His tail twitched back and forth as if he was thinking over what she said. His black nose quivered. He edged closer.

Buck's dark upper lip pulled the corn and a piece of the carrot into his mouth. "Good boy." At this

close range, Bits could see the light and dark hairs around his muzzle ripple as he chewed. When he finished, he raised his head even with hers. Please, don't let him hear a noise and bolt, Bits prayed silently. Buck's black nostrils widened as he smelled the apple in her hand.

"You can do it," she coaxed.

He remained still, studying her. For weeks Bits had waited and planned for this moment, but now that it was here she didn't know how to make it happen. Seconds ticked by. Please take the apple, she thought as hard as she could. Buck's large eyes burned into her. Then bit by bit he lowered his head.

He was going to do it! Her heart pounded inside her chest. Six inches. She could feel his breath on her palm. Two inches.

The apple wobbled in her hand, and the soft hairs under his chin tickled her fingers.

"You're beautiful," she breathed.

He retreated a couple of feet to chew the apple. She watched his jaw make the circular motion she'd grown to love.

He was bolder the second time. Bits felt tiny hairs again, but this time instead of pulling back, he just raised his head. As he reached for the last chunk of apple, Bits inched her empty hand off her knee.

"I just want to pet you," she pleaded. She left her hand in midair. "Please?"

Buck eyed her warily and took a step to his left before lowering his head again. With her index and middle fingers outstretched, Bits moved her hand toward him. He didn't pull away. Holding her breath, she touched the area above his nose. It was slightly oily, and she could feel bone underneath. Gently she stroked the bridge of his nose.

"I'll always be your friend," she whispered. "Always."

Buck snatched the last piece of apple from her hand, then backed out of her reach. She knew he would leave now. That was okay. They had all the time in the world.

When Bits didn't see Chris in the hall the next morning, she went to look for her in Mr. Fritch's homeroom. She wasn't there either.

"Chris has a dentist appointment at 9:30," said a voice behind her. Bits whirled around. Jeremy was standing two feet away, his sandy hair falling every which way.

"Oh." Bits shrugged. "I was just going to tell her something." She didn't want him thinking she was desperate or anything.

"Mom's bringing her later."

Bits was surprised. Why was he being so friendly? She eyed him carefully. Was this a set-up for some kind of practical joke? He stood there waiting for her to say something. Suddenly his attention shifted

down the hall. Bits followed his gaze. Travis was on the steps, urgently motioning for Jeremy to join him.

"Gotta go," he said, and hurried away.

Something was up. Bits could feel it. She'd have to ask Chris what those two were up to now.

At lunch, Bits wound her way through a maze of chairs to sit with Chris. Her lopsided smile reminded Bits of her own visits to the dentist. She wondered if Mom had found them a new one yet.

"Do you like your dentist?" asked Bits, sitting down.

"Yeah," answered Chris. "The worst thing is the novocaine shot." She looked at Bits. "How'd you know I was at the dentist?"

"Jeremy told me."

Chris nodded. "I'm still a little numb. Hope I don't spill milk all over myself." She raised the carton and took a swallow, but nothing ran down her chin.

"Do you have any pets?" asked Bits, taking a bite of her chicken chow mein.

"A dog. His name is Pooch. We've got a cat, too—Smudgy. She sleeps with me every night. Chickens too, but they don't count."

"How come?" asked Bits.

Just then, Jeremy came over and plopped down next to his sister. "Hi."

"Who invited you?" asked Chris.

"I did." answered Jeremy. "What are you talking about?" His eyes scanned the room.

Bits didn't see Travis, but she noticed Julie and Karen two tables away.

"Chickens," answered Chris.

"B-w-a-k, b-w-a-k," cackled Jeremy.

Chris rolled her eyes.

He licked his lips. "I *love* chicken."

"Why aren't they pets?" asked Bits.

"Because this weekend we're going to butcher them," answered Chris.

Bits swallowed. "Butcher?"

"Yeah," piped in Jeremy. "You whack their heads off with an ax, then watch them flop around."

Bits stared at her plate of chicken chow mein.

Chris elbowed her brother.

"What?"

"You're being gross," said Chris. "Besides, *you* don't kill them, you just pluck the feathers."

"I'm the fastest feather plucker in Wisconsin," Jeremy boasted.

Bits lowered her fork to her plate. She didn't feel hungry anymore.

Julie and Karen got up to leave. "Oh, oh," said Jeremy. "See you."

"What are you and Travis up to?" asked Chris.

"Just a little payback for the Super Glue Julie squeezed into Travis's locker this morning." He tore out the door.

"You kill the chickens?" asked Bits.

Chris gave her an "are you still on that" look. "Well, yeah. I'd much rather do that than pluck feathers."

"But how can you . . . do that?" Bits couldn't imagine killing anything. Bugs maybe, but not real animals.

"Don't you *eat* chicken?" Chris asked as if there was something wrong with Bits.

"Yes, but that's not the same," Bits protested.

"Well, where do you think the chickens come from?" asked Chris. "At least ours get to run around in the yard instead of being trapped in some dinky cage all the time."

Bits didn't say anything. Maybe she'd give up eating chicken, become a vegetarian instead. Shanti and her family were vegetarians.

Chris waved her hand in front of Bits's face.

"What?"

"Let's go see what Jeremy and Travis are up to."

In the hallway, Mr. Grant, the assistant principal, was inspecting the inside of Julie's locker door. Thick white streaks ran down the entire length of the door.

"They must've used Elmer's glue," said Chris, shaking her head. "Dummies!"

"Why?" asked Bits. "Julie did it to Travis, didn't she?"

"Because it's so obvious," said Chris. "The Super

Glue Julie used was transparent. Travis probably didn't know anything was wrong until he touched his locker. And now that Mr. Grant has seen this"—she pointed to Julie's locker—"we'll probably have to do some extra assignment or something."

Chris's prophecy came true later that afternoon. When no one came forward to admit responsibility for the glue, both seventh-grade homerooms were given additional assignments. Mr. Fritch handed out an extra sheet of algebra problems, and Mrs. Carlson passed around a correct-the-grammar page.

Bits groaned along with the rest of the class. Some of the kids gave Travis and Jeremy dirty looks, but Bits thought Julie should be getting those looks. After all she'd started the whole thing.

Bits wished she could think of something that would take Julie down a notch or two. She twisted her rhinestone earring between her fingers. What if she tripped in the lunchroom and dumped an entire plate of macaroni and tomato sauce all over Julie? No, too obvious. She'd have to think of something else. Whatever she did, she'd have to be careful. Julie had a talent for coming out on top, and Bits didn't want to end up on the bottom end of her own prank.

9

"I'm having lunch with some people I met at the Save the Rivers meeting last Saturday," said Mom, putting on her coat. "I should be back around 2:30. I'll stop and get groceries on the way home. Want anything special?"

Bits smiled as she imagined the look on Mom's face if she asked for a fifty-pound bag of shelled corn. She shook her head no.

"Apples?" asked Mom.

"Sure." The extra fruit would help, but Bits was still going to have to make another trip to the store. Her cache was almost gone.

"Call your dad if anything comes up." Mom dawdled in the front hall. Bits wanted to push her out the door and into the car. The sooner she left, the earlier she'd be back. Then Bits could go see Buck.

At last Mom shut the door, leaving Bits and Jason alone.

"Hey, Jase," called Bits. "Did you hear your big

sister has a deer eating out of her hand?" Jason looked at her. "You didn't?" He threw a string of pull-apart toys out of the playpen, then started crying. "Guess you're not too impressed, are you?" Bits bent over to pick up the toys and tossed them back into the playpen.

It was hard not to share her excitement about Buck with anyone. Maybe Celie was home. Bits lifted the phone, then put it back down again. On second thought, Celie would just say "that's great" about Buck, then move on to what was going on in Chicago. Reading Celie's letter last week, Bits had been keenly aware of how different their lives were becoming. Celie would never be able to understand how excited Bits felt when Buck finally ate from her hand, or how she loved to see small areas of his coat shiver where a fly landed. She shook her head. She'd have to find someone else to share Buck with.

After lunch Bits put the dirty dishes in the sink. She bundled up Jason and buckled him into the back carrier. A walk would help the afternoon pass.

Instead of taking the trail, Bits took a shortcut through the young tree plantation next to their property. Baby Norway pines, just two or three feet tall, grew in sandy furrows.

She scanned the clearing ahead just in case Buck was in the area. In her heart she knew it was way too early to see him, but it didn't hurt to check.

Back on the trail, Jason was bored in the back-

pack. He fussed, squirmed around, and pulled her hair. "Ouch!" Bits knelt and picked up a small gray-white branch. It looked like driftwood except for the marks where larvae had tunneled their way under the bark. "Here." She handed it to Jason. "Just don't eat it, okay?"

There were a couple of holes burrowed into the bank of the trail, and Bits wondered what creature was tucked away inside them. She scrambled up the opposite bank. On her right near the top of the rise was a clearing. An old rusted pail caught Bits's eye. She waded through the grass to investigate. Metal bedsprings, an old-fashioned bike frame, and a stuffed chair were half-hidden by grass and scrub. Bits was annoyed. Why hadn't people taken this stuff to a dump somewhere? Why mess up the woods?

Trudging through the soft sand on the trail, Bits spotted deer tracks. The tracks disappeared into the brush. Were they Buck's? Bits wished she had paid more attention to his hoof prints.

Another trail led into the woods on the far side of the clearing. Bits headed down it. No branches lay on the ground here. Thick brush lined both sides of the path. Where the trail turned north, Bits spotted more trash in the grass. Beer cans.

"Jerks," she muttered. She'd collect the cans on the way back home.

She entered another tree plantation. Here the

Norway pines were twenty-five feet tall, stretching in straight lines for as far as Bits could see. A carpet of dried red pine needles covered the ground. Bits ducked low under the boughs. Jason's added weight unbalanced her as she stood up again.

Bits retreated again to the trail where walking was easier. Jason's breathing was slow and even. He had fallen asleep.

Just ahead were two jack pines almost totally stripped of their bark. One of them swayed mysteriously back and forth. Bits looked up. Near the top of the tree sat a fat porcupine munching away.

"Am I interrupting your lunch?" she called.

At her voice, the porcupine raised his spines.

"Hey, that's okay," said Bits. "I'm leaving."

Dad had warned her about porcupine quills. *"Bon appétit,"* she called, or should it be bark appétit? She shrugged and continued on.

Suddenly Bits stopped short. Had one of the tangled limbs in the brush pile ahead really moved or had she just imagined it?

"Buck?" she called uncertainly. "What are you doing back here?" Good grief, she thought. She was talking to him as if she expected him to answer. Jason wiggled in the carrier. "Don't wake up now," she groaned.

Buck's head shot up and his ears turned as far back as they could.

"What's wrong?"

He bolted into the woods.

Then Bits heard it, too. A low rumble in the distance that grew louder every second. She crouched down behind a tree trunk. She'd never heard an engine like this before. Peeking around the tree, she waited.

The rumble became a roar. Jason started to cry. "Sh-hh," said Bits. "I'm scared, too. We'll go home as soon as they pass."

Two four-wheelers whipped down the trail. Their tires bounced off the ground each time the huge wheels hit a bump. Two young men dressed in green camouflage suits steered the vehicles. As they zoomed past Bits, she noticed long rectangular cases strapped behind the drivers' seats.

Then they disappeared. The engine noise seemed to take forever to fade away. Only then did Bits feel safe enough to leave her hiding spot and hurry home.

10

The next day Mom and Dad took Bits and Jason to the Twin Ports, Duluth and Superior. They ate out, then shopped near Lake Superior. It was rainy, and fog hung over the big lake like a heavy wool blanket.

Bits spotted the earrings immediately. The silver deer-shapes glinted under the nature store's track lighting. Two tiny Bucks, except that the earrings had an extra tine on each antler. She couldn't help staring at them.

Dad came up behind her. "Whoever made these knows animals." He fingered the silver deer.

Bits nodded. She longed to buy them, but they were fifteen dollars. If she bought them, then she wouldn't have any money to buy food for Buck.

"You haven't had new earrings in a while, have you?" asked Dad.

"Don't get anywhere to buy any."

Bits caught the pained look in Dad's eyes and felt

awful. But she hadn't meant anything, she was just telling the truth.

"Excuse me," said Dad, getting the clerk's attention. "We'd like to buy these. Oh, and this pair, too." Bits smiled. She'd wear them to school tomorrow.

"Boo!" said Jeremy, as he and Chris came up behind Bits.

Chris leaned against the next locker. "I keep hoping he's a ghost, and someday he'll disappear."

"Very funny," said Jeremy.

Bits grinned at the two of them. She liked the way they teased each other.

"You have new earrings," said Chris.

She'd noticed!

"Neat deer. What's the other one?"

"Porcupine quill," answered Bits.

"Really?" Chris reached out for the thin shaft. It was dark near the top, and a cream color toward the tip.

Jeremy elbowed his sister.

"Okay, okay," said Chris. "Would you like to go trick-or-treating with us on Friday?"

Bits hadn't really thought much about Halloween, though Mom had brought home a pumpkin on Saturday and they had carved it later that day.

"Our dad's taking us into town," said Jeremy.

"It'll be Jeremy, Lisa, you and me," said Chris.

"Sounds like fun," said Bits. "I've never gone door to door before. In the city you go to parties instead."

"We'll make a real haul," said Jeremy. He rubbed his hands together. "Enough to last six months."

"Six months?" Bits eyes widened. "You get that much?"

"No," said Chris. "We get a lot, but Mom only lets us have a few pieces at a time. She puts the rest away. If she didn't, Garbage Pit here would eat it all up in two days."

"Would not," protested Jeremy. "Hey, there's Travis. See ya." He hurried away.

"What are you going to wear?" asked Chris.

Bits thought about it. "I have the tail and ears from my costume last year. I was a cat. How about you?"

"I'm going to be a waitress. My mom still has the uniform she wore when she worked at the cafe. Lisa's going as an angel, but don't believe it. I keep telling Jeremy he should go as a pig."

Bits laughed. It felt good to laugh with Chris.

The bell went off.

"Bring a pillowcase along for the goodies," said Chris. "Maybe we can ditch Lisa and Jeremy and go off by ourselves." She glanced toward Fritch's room. "See you at lunch."

"I can't," said Bits. "I'm going to the store."

Chris wrinkled her forehead. "What for?"

"I have to pick up some stuff for my mom." Bits could tell from Chris's face that she didn't believe her. But Chris just shrugged, then disappeared into her homeroom. Bits shook her head. She'd have to tell someone about Buck soon. All these white lies were starting to bother her.

At noon Bits forced herself to walk casually out the door. She was more nervous today than last week. What if someone realized she wasn't a townie and squealed? Well, she'd just have to take that chance.

The store was busier today, and an elderly couple blocked the aisle to the produce section. Bits scurried down another aisle, past the dairy cases. Cold air leaked out at her. There was a waist-high meat case in front of her. Butchers dressed in white stood working at stainless steel tables behind a glass partition.

"Gross me out," moaned Bits.

Three full-sized beef carcasses hung from hooks, the meat beet red, with jagged lines of dull white tallow running the length of the bodies. She'd never seen meat this way before—only neatly cut up and wrapped in plastic.

She reached the produce section, grabbed food for Buck, then hurried into the back room. Now there were apple-flavored mineral blocks next to the

salt licks. She wanted one, but they weighed twenty-five pounds. She scooped corn into a plastic bag and ran toward the checkout. It was twenty after twelve. She had ten minutes to make it back on time.

Bits yanked the school door open. The halls were empty. In the distance a locker door slammed shut. The bell had gone off. There wasn't time to go to her own locker now.

As she staggered down the hall, Mr. Grant came out of the boy's bathroom. Oh, no! she thought. If he sees me, I'm dead! Someone must have heard her silent prayer. Mr. Grant headed toward his office without a backward glance.

Bits slipped into Mr. Fritch's room. She felt his annoyance, but he just motioned her to her seat. She slid along the wall and dropped into her chair. Bits knew her face was bright red.

Jeremy, who sat a row over and one seat ahead, wrote something on his notebook, then showed it to her. "We're having a quiz." He smiled.

Bits smiled back. Maybe Jeremy wasn't such a jerk after all.

Buck had showed up every day but Tuesday that week, and last night he'd even let Bits stroke his cheek and neck while he nibbled the food in her hand.

Today she leaned against the weathered ladder as

Buck ambled toward her. She loved watching the slight dip his neck and head made every time he took a step.

"You walk like a dancer," said Bits, when he stopped in front of her. He lifted his head even with hers and peered at her like some kind of inspector.

"Yes, I have food, but you have to find it."

He immediately zeroed in on the food in her pockets as if he'd understood her. Bits didn't move while he pushed gently on the material with his muzzle. Still she kept her hands in her pockets. He gazed up at her and let out a low, throaty sound.

Bits blinked. "Was that you?"

Buck repeated the short, deep call.

"You *can* talk."

"M-m-nn!" He was more insistent this time as he pushed against her pocket.

"Okay, okay," chuckled Bits. She pulled out her hand and offered him two carrot halves. He ate them quickly. She brought out an apple then and sliced it. Again he talked to her.

"You're telling me to hurry up, aren't you?" She shook her forefinger at him. "I've got a good mind not to give you any apple since you're so impatient," she teased. He lifted his black nose to smell her finger. She felt warm puffs of air as he exhaled, and her heart melted. She held a wedge of apple out to him. He took the fruit from her hand hungrily.

"Guess what?" She fed him another piece. "I'm

going trick-or-treating with Chris and Jeremy tonight. Bet you didn't know it was Halloween."

A chunk of apple fell from his mouth.

"Now don't slobber so much," she chided. "I
almost got caught getting this stuff for you."

Buck stopped chewing. His left ear twitched to
the side, then just as quickly relaxed, and he continued chewing.

"You know what? I think Jeremy likes me. He
didn't have to tell me there was going to be a test."

Buck nuzzled her other pocket. Bits pulled out a
bag of corn and emptied it into her hand. Buck
dragged the hard kernels into his mouth with his
upper lip.

She stroked him between his eyes. Would he let
her touch his antlers? Slowly she reached up to ca-
ress a smooth, cream-colored tip. Buck pulled his
head out of her reach.

"Don't want me to touch them, do you?" Disappointed, she settled for stroking his cheek.

The food was gone but Buck continued to smell
her hands.

"There isn't any more food," said Bits.

His pink tongue darted out, grazing her hand. Bits
yanked her hand away out of reflex. Then she held
it out to him. Again the pink tongue flickered over
her skin—soft yet firm, and moist. When he finished with the palm of her hand, he started on the
back.

Bits raised her other hand to her lips and tasted the skin. "You're after the salt, aren't you?"

Bits ruffled the soft coat covering his neck. The outer fur was brown with grey tips, but whitish closer to his skin.

"What would you think about me bringing Chris to see you?" She massaged the tendons and muscles under his coat. "I wouldn't let her scare you or anything. If you didn't like her, I wouldn't bring her again." She paused. "Should we try it?"

She brushed her nose against his fur. He smelled of earth and pine. "It'll be okay," she said. "I promise."

11

hris had said they'd stop by and pick Bits up around 6:30. At twenty to seven headlights danced down the uneven driveway.

Bits slipped into her jacket. A cat's tail curled out from underneath. She had drawn whiskers from her mouth across her cheeks with her mom's eyebrow pencil and circled her eyes and nose with purplish eyeshadow.

Bits opened the front door. Dad followed her outside. A long pickup pulled into the turnaround by the house. In the glow of the yard light, it reminded Bits of the trucks city workers in Chicago used. Mr. Howard and Jeremy sat in front. Chris and Lisa were behind them in the back seat.

Mr. Howard rolled down his window. "Nice to meet you," he said. "Heard a lot about your daughter here."

"Glad to meet you," said Bits's father. They shook hands.

Bits read the words "City of Superior" on the door, encircling a faded emblem. Below it were patches of rust. She shivered. The temperature was dropping, and the thin leotard she wore underneath her jacket wasn't very warm.

Jeremy jumped out of the passenger side. "Come on."

He had drawn a beard on his chin and covered one eye with a pirate's patch. Bits hurried to the door. Jeremy flopped the seat forward, and she climbed onto the bench in back next to Chris.

"This is Lisa," said Chris.

"Hi," said Bits.

The six-year-old stared at Bits, but didn't return her greeting. Her halo tipped to one side.

"You're leaning," said Bits.

Lisa didn't stop staring but pushed the wire halo straight again.

"Is she okay?" whispered Bits.

"Yeah," answered Chris. "She didn't believe me when I told her you wore three earrings in one ear."

Mr. Howard revved the truck's engine and backed out of the turnaround. The rusty muffler echoed loudly among the trees. The truck's interior smelled of sweat and wood. On the truck bed behind were scattered split logs and a couple of yellow plastic bottles with the word "Heet" printed on them.

"Neat costume," said Jeremy.

Bits hadn't realized he was looking at her.

"Yeah," agreed Chris.

"Thanks," said Bits. She wondered how they could tell with her jacket on. Maybe they meant her makeup.

Chris's costume was a too-big white dress and a black apron. Lisa wore a white sheet with wings pinned on the back.

The truck bounced onto the road. Bits was excited. She'd never ridden in a pickup truck. She peered out the side window down the dark country road. There wasn't a moon, but she could see lots of stars.

Suddenly the truck slowed. Ahead on the right, two eyes glowed amber in the darkness.

"It's a deer," said Jeremy.

The truck slowed down even more. "A doe," added Mr. Howard.

The animal darted onto the roadway, then stood still, hypnotized by the bright lights.

"You can never be sure which way they'll go," said Mr. Howard, hitting the brake. Bits could see him in the eerie green light cast by the dashboard. He was thin and light haired like Jeremy.

"Sometimes you think they'll go across, then they do just the opposite." As he spoke the doe retreated back the way she'd come.

"Went into the ditch more than once trying to avoid one." Mr. Howard scratched his beard. "If

81

you ask me there's getting to be too many road kills in the area." The truck accelerated again.

"Didn't see any fawns with her," said Jeremy, peering out the window.

Bits shuddered. She hoped Buck stayed in the woods. At least the road past their place wasn't very busy.

When they came to town, the bright streetlights hurt Bits's eyes. She didn't think they were any brighter than the streetlights in Chicago. Maybe she was getting used to the darkness up here.

Mr. Howard steered the truck around a corner, then pulled over to the side of the street. "Here we are," he said, shifting the truck into neutral. "I'm going down to the Trapper Bar. I'll meet you back here in an hour and a half. If you get cold before then, come down and get me."

Jeremy climbed out and flopped the seat forward for Bits, Chris, and Lisa. The truck pulled away.

"Let's hit this side first," suggested Jeremy.

"Okay by me," said Chris.

Bits and Chris let Jeremy and Lisa lead the way. The bottom of Lisa's costume dragged on the ground, and she was having a hard time keeping up with her older brother.

"You never went door to door in the city?" asked Chris.

"I went to parties at someone's house or at the Y. Even the school had something."

"We have a party in the gymnasium for the little kids," said Chris.

"I know," said Bits. "I saw the sign-up sheet." Seventh-and-eighth graders could sign up to run booths for the younger kids. Maybe next year she'd do that.

Jeremy and Lisa knocked on the first door.

"We better get up there," said Chris. They bounded up the walk to the steps.

"Trick-or-treat!" they all chimed as the door opened. They held out their pillowcases to receive the first batch of goodies.

They'd finished one street and were heading down another. Several carved pumpkins lined one sidewalk. Inside each gourd a candle burned.

"Will the deer eat these pumpkins?" asked Lisa.

"Probably not," answered Chris. "But the ones we have at home will probably be gone tomorrow."

"Deer eat pumpkins?" asked Bits.

"Yeah," answered Jeremy.

"They knock the tops off with their hooves," added Chris, "so they can bite into the hole."

Bits nodded. Now she knew what to do with the pumpkin she and Mom had carved.

The light from the candles flickered prettily on the walk.

"These people *really* get into Halloween," whispered Chris. "You wait and see."

Jeremy rang the doorbell, and the door burst

open. There stood a six-foot-tall gorilla. He was making grunting sounds.

Lisa screamed and hid behind Chris. The gorilla scratched his head and knelt down. He beckoned to Lisa. When she didn't come, he whimpered.

"Go on," said Chris, pulling Lisa out from behind her. "You're hurting his feelings. He thinks you don't like him."

With Chris behind her, Lisa inched her way forward. The gorilla made cooing sounds. Lisa got to arm's length, then held out her pillowcase. The gorilla dropped something in her bag and Lisa hid behind Chris again.

When Bits stepped up for her treat, the gorilla stood up, let out a Tarzan yell, and started beating his chest.

Bits tried not to giggle. She heard a woman's voice from inside the house.

"Honey, don't scare the poor kids."

The gorilla shrugged and dropped something into her pillowcase.

Now it was Jeremy's turn. The gorilla put up his fists as if he were going to fight. Jeremy played the game and bopped him on the chin. The gorilla staggered backward, and they all laughed.

"That's the best house," said Chris, as they walked back past the dancing lights cast by the jack-o'-lanterns. "Every year he dresses up in a different costume."

"Who is that?" asked Bits.

"Mr. Swanson," answered Jeremy. "He owns the hardware store." He unwrapped something from his bag. "He's giving everyone a dollar again." Jeremy held up the crisp dollar bill that had been slipped under a chocolate bar wrapper.

"A dollar!" Lisa's eyes grew big. She searched her pillowcase for the money.

Chris and Bits walked ahead while Jeremy stopped to help Lisa look for her dollar. Gradually the two girls got farther and farther ahead. Chris turned and looked back at her brother and sister, and Bits followed her gaze. Jeremy was on his knees, and Lisa had her arm around him.

"Come on, you slowpokes," Bits yelled.

"Don't," snapped Chris.

"I was just teasing. . . . " But Chris didn't hear. She was hurrying back to Jeremy and Lisa. Bits followed. Then she heard Jeremy wheezing.

Chris picked up the candy wrapper lying next to Jeremy's feet. "You ate nuts?"

Jeremy nodded as he tried to take a breath.

"Where's your inhaler?" asked Chris.

"I don't"—wheeze—"have it."

Chris groaned.

"I don't need"—wheeze—"to carry it"—wheeze—"anymore," he said stubbornly.

Bits didn't know what was going on. "Inhaler?"

"Yeah," answered Chris. "He has asthma. Nuts

trigger an attack." She looked at Lisa. "Have you got your inhaler?"

"Mom put it in my coat pocket."

"Here," said Chris. She pushed her pillowcase into Bits's hands.

Bits watched her lift up Lisa's costume and frantically search the coat pockets.

"Here it is," said Chris. She pulled out a plastic canister and handed it to Jeremy.

Jeremy clapped the inhaler over his mouth and squeezed the canister. His breathing quieted.

"Lisa has asthma, too," said Chris, taking her pillowcase back.

"Here," said Jeremy. He shoved the inhaler into Lisa's hands, then brushed by Bits.

She looked at Chris.

"He hates it when someone sees him have an attack," explained Chris.

Bits didn't understand. So what if he had asthma?

Jeremy's attack had dampened their spirits, and now they all began to feel the near-freezing temperature. Bits could see their breath.

"I'm cold," complained Lisa.

"Me, too," agreed Bits.

"Let's go to the Trapper," called Chris.

Jeremy was twenty feet ahead of them. He turned toward Main Street. Soon they were in the truck headed for home.

"Can you come and stay overnight sometime next week?" asked Bits when she'd warmed up.

"I can't Monday, Wednesday, or Thursday," said Chris. "Mom works at the grocery store those nights, and I have to baby-sit Lisa."

"No you don't," piped up the six-year-old. "I don't need a baby-sitter." She snuggled into Chris.

"How about Friday?" asked Bits.

"I'll ask," said Chris. She raised her voice over the motor. "Dad, can I stay overnight at Bits's next Friday?"

Mr. Howard was silent a minute. "Don't see any reason why not."

"Great!" Bits was glad Chris could come over. Now she'd be able to show her Buck.

"Do you think . . . " Chris stopped, then took a deep breath. "Do you think we could pierce one of my ears?" The words rushed out.

"Sure," said Bits. "I'm pretty good at piercing ears." She'd done her own second and third holes; she'd done Kersten's ears, too.

Chris sighed. "Better not."

"Why?"

"I don't have any earrings."

"You can wear one of mine," said Bits. "I have lots I don't wear anymore."

"Really?"

Bits nodded.

"Are you going to wear that rhinestone one anymore?" asked Chris.

Bits thought about it. "I haven't decided yet. I didn't get that one too long ago."

"Oh."

Bits could tell Chris was disappointed with her answer, but she liked that earring. "I have another really cool one you might like."

"Great," said Chris.

"What?" asked a sleepy Lisa.

"Never mind," said Chris.

Bits smiled. Maybe the two of them could be friends as good as she and Celie had been.

The next evening the temperature dropped below freezing. Bits basked in the warmth radiating from the woodstove, her arms folded around her knees. She gazed at the logs burning behind the glass door. The last flame had sputtered out several minutes ago. Now the logs were covered with a hot ash that glowed red, faded, then glowed again.

She went to the woodbin to retrieve more firewood, but found only a couple of logs. With Dad working so much overtime lately, the job of filling the woodbin had fallen to her.

"Going to get wood," she called.

Bits stood on the back steps for a few seconds while her eyes adjusted to the darkness. She hated turning on the yard light because then she couldn't

see the stars as well. Soon she picked out the sandy soil of the driveway. She ventured down the drive to an open spot.

Above her, the large band of the Milky Way stars peppered the sky. Bits didn't think she'd ever seen this many stars before. Certainly never in Chicago. She tipped her head back as far as it could go and slowly turned around. What was that? A shining object was moving slowly across the sky. It wasn't a star, or a plane, either—their lights always blinked.

"A satellite," breathed Bits. It had to be.

A twig snapped in the woods. Bits peered into the darkness, but didn't see anything. She smiled. Six weeks ago a sound like that would have sent her scurrying back into the house and the safety of her bedroom.

A streak of light arched across the sky—a shooting star. Bits caught her breath.

It was funny how things went. If she still lived in the city, she'd never have seen all this. She'd never have tamed Buck, either. She felt a warmth spread inside her. She was beginning to feel glad they had moved.

12

Friday afternoon when Bits and Chris jumped off the bus, Chris turned to Bits. "Okay," she said, "now tell me what the surprise is." It was the third time she'd tried to get Bits to tell her.

"No," said Bits.

Chris groaned. "I hate waiting." Her braid bounced from side to side on her back. "Whenever I ask my mom about something important she says wait until next year. Dad says wait until you're older. Larry says wait until you're in high school, hah-hah-hah. I'm going to end up being ninety years old and still waiting!"

Bits laughed. "I won't make you wait that long, just another half hour."

They reached the house, and Bits opened the door. "Mom?"

"Right here." She came into the kitchen with Jason in her arms.

"This is Chris."

"Nice to meet you," said Mom.

"Hi," said Chris.

"And that's my baby brother, Jason," added Bits. "I'll be right back." She hurried into her room and pulled Buck's food out from under the bed. She stuffed her pockets, then returned to the kitchen.

While Bits was digging in the refrigerator, Chris leaned over beside her. "Are you still going to pierce my ear?" she whispered.

"Not yet," answered Bits. A look of relief flashed across Chris's face. "Later, after the surprise." She grabbed two apples. "Then we'll do it."

Chris nodded and followed Bits to the door.

"Where are you going?" asked Mom.

"For a walk," answered Bits.

"Don't be late for dinner," she called.

"We won't." The door banged closed behind them.

"So where *are* we going?" asked Chris.

"Someplace special," answered Bits. She held out an apple. "Want one of these?"

"Sure," answered Chris.

Bits hurried them toward the iron pipe marking the property line.

"Who lives next to you?" asked Chris.

"Nobody. It's a tree plantation that belongs to the paper company."

"My dad works for them sometimes," said Chris. "Once in a while they need extra loggers." She drew

her arm back to throw her half-eaten apple into the woods.

"Wait!" said Bits. "I need that."

"You need my apple core?" Chris gave her a funny look. "How come?"

"You'll see."

Chris groaned. "There you go again. Just wait . . . later . . . you'll see. . . . "

Bits laughed and danced down the trail ahead of her friend. Not far from the ladder, she turned and waited for Chris. "Shut your eyes," said Bits.

"What?"

"Close your eyes," she insisted.

Chris folded her arms across her chest. "Why?"

"Because it won't be a surprise if your eyes are open."

Chris thought it over. "Okay." She snapped her eyelids closed.

Bits took her hand and led her to the ladder. "Sit down," she commanded, and helped Chris sit crossed-legged on the ground. "Behind you there's a board to lean against, but don't open your eyes yet."

Chris made a face. Bits rubbed the two apple cores against the birch's trunk. Then, she fanned the air to help the breeze carry the apple scent away from the clearing.

Next she emptied her pockets. She had already

decided how to put the food out; the broken carrot halves four feet away from Chris, the corn kernels two feet away. This way Buck could get used to Chris gradually just like he'd gotten used to her. She kept the apple wedges in her pocket. If things went the way she planned, Buck might be brave enough to eat out of her hand. Bits plopped down next to Chris.

"Can I open my eyes yet?" complained Chris.

"Pretty soon." She scanned the edge of the clearing. No Buck.

Chris felt behind her. "What is this?"

"A ladder."

Chris frowned. "A ladder out in the woods?" She reached up until she felt the bottom rung. "Can't I open my eyes? Whatever it is, I promise I'll be surprised."

"No," said Bits. She twisted a piece of brown grass in her fingers. What if Buck didn't show up? It wasn't windy or rainy. He'll come, she reassured herself. She felt Chris move. "You opened your eyes."

"Good thing, too," said Chris. "I'd have stabbed myself on this." She held out a thin, three-inch sliver of wood.

Bits saw the fresh scar in the first ladder rung.

"Great deer stand," said Chris, looking up.

"Is that what it's called?"

Chris nodded.

"What do people do, feed the deer and sit and watch them eat?"

Chris laughed. "That's a good one, Bits."

"What?"

Something rustled the branches to their left.

Chris stopped smiling. "You're serious, aren't you?"

"Ssh-h," said Bits. She took the apple pieces from her pocket.

Buck entered the clearing near the fallen log. His ears twitched back and forth. He hesitated. Bits knew he'd picked up Chris's scent.

"Is he the surprise?"

"Yes." Bits whispered. Buck moved closer, bobbing his head up and down. "I've tamed him." She was talking softly, but the pride she felt still crept into her words.

"You have?"

"Keep your voice down," said Bits. "He's used to me talking to him, but with you here he's going to be more nervous than usual."

"How did you tame him?" asked Chris.

"I used food," she answered, "and if you don't scare him you might see him eat out of my hand."

"You're kidding."

Bits smiled at Chris's disbelief. She was impressed!

94

"I've never seen a live deer this close. He's kinda cute."

Kinda cute! Bits rolled her eyes. This wasn't some boy they were talking about. This was Buck. Buck, who let her sink her hands into his soft, thick coat. Who gently licked her fingers clean. He wasn't cute. He was beautiful.

Buck took a stiff-legged step toward the carrot, then stretched his neck to reach it. His ears swiveled toward every new sound. His eyes never left Chris.

"Bits—"

The alarm she heard in Chris's voice startled Bits.

"You're wrong about people using deer stands to watch deer eat."

"Well, what are they used for then?" Bits asked, her eyes on Buck. Why couldn't Chris wait until after he left to tell her this? He'd finished eating the carrot and was stretching his head toward the corn.

"Hunters sit up there," Chris said finally.

"So?"

Buck inched closer and scooped the yellow kernels into his mouth.

"Don't you get it?"

Buck jerked his head up and backed away.

Now look what Chris had done! "What does this have to do with my deer?" Bits demanded. Why did she suddenly have the feeling that something awful was lurking nearby?

Chris shook her head. "Bits, deer season opens three weeks from tomorrow. This isn't a deserted deer stand; it's in too good shape. I'll bet hunters use this every year."

Hunters! Bits whipped around to face Chris. "Are—are you saying he could get killed if he comes here?"

Buck shied away, turned and watched them.

"Finally you understand!"

The vision of Buck hanging from a meat hook propelled Bits to her feet. "No-o-o. It can't be true!"

Chris jumped up next to her.

Buck bounded into the forest and disappeared.

"Bits, I'm telling you the truth. You've done exactly what hunters do—put bait out near a deer stand to attract game. Unless you do something, your deer has a real good chance of getting shot."

Bits flinched. "I—I didn't know. How could I?" She looked at Chris helplessly. "What am I going to do?"

Chris shook her head. "I don't know. Up here, everybody hunts. There's so many guns going off that first weekend, it's like the Fourth of July."

"Is there only one weekend of deer hunting?" Maybe Mom and Dad would let her camp out here. Then she could chase away any hunter that came near the clearing. What was she thinking? They had guns. What did she have? Nothing!

"The season is usually nine days," said Chris,

"but this year there are so many deer, the Department of Natural Resources added seven more days."

"Sixteen days!" Her parents would never let her stay out here that long. What was she going to do? She didn't know anything about hunting. She eyed Chris. "How come you know so much about hunting?"

Chris hesitated. "My dad and Larry hunt. Jeremy might go this year, too."

Bits panicked. "You won't tell them about this spot, will you?"

"No," answered Chris. "You don't have to worry about us; we always hunt south of our place."

Bits reached out to lean against the deer stand, but at the last second she yanked her hand away.

"You okay?" asked Chris.

"Yes," Bits stammered, rubbing her forehead. She searched her friend's face. What had Chris meant— "You don't have to worry about *us?*" Bits was afraid to ask. "Do you go along, too?"

Chris didn't say anything.

"Well, do you?"

"I have my Hunter's Education Certificate from the DNR," answered Chris.

"Oh." That still didn't answer her question. Bits remembered when Chris had told her about killing the chickens. "Have you ever shot anything?"

Chris dug her fingers into her pockets.

"You have, haven't you? How could you! What was it?"

"Bits, let's just forget it."

"No." She had to know.

Chris sighed. "I shot a rabbit."

"A rabbit!" Bits stared at her. She had held soft, furry rabbits in her arms. "How could you do that?" She felt sick with disgust.

"Look," snapped Chris. "Dad and Larry were away last summer helping my grandpa on his farm, and this huge rabbit kept getting into the garden. He was eating everything. Jeremy tried to get it a couple of times, but he missed. So I got him. Okay?"

No, it wasn't okay. Not with Bits. "I don't believe it. I'm friends with someone who kills chickens and rabbits. I suppose in three weeks you'll go after some poor deer."

Chris was silent.

"You *are* going, aren't you?"

"I've asked my dad to take me along." Chris squared her shoulders.

"You're weird, you know that? And to think I thought we could be friends!"

"You don't understand," said Chris. "Hunting helps the deer."

Bits didn't hear her. All the loneliness of the past few weeks clenched into one big fist inside her. She took a menacing step towards Chris. "Tell me," she snarled, "do you *like* killing things?"

Chris backed away.

"I bet you enjoy seeing all that blood and guts!"

Chris turned and hurried away.

"Butcher! Killer!" Bits shouted after her.

Chris disappeared into the trees. Bits turned to glare at the deer stand. She kicked a branch out of her way, then scooped it up and slammed it against the side support. The branch snapped in two, the top half flying into the brush. Bits flung the rest aside. Tears rolled down her cheeks. "No!" She scrubbed them away with her coat sleeve. There wasn't time to cry. She had to think. She had to protect Buck from people like Chris.

13

Bits didn't go home until it was almost dark. She spent the afternoon storming around the woods, half of her wanting to see Buck, the other half dreading that she would see him. The yard light cast a yellowish haze over the garage and the turnaround. She hoped one of her parents had taken Chris home. Seeing her friend—make that ex-friend—would only confuse her more.

She opened the door.

"You had us worried." Dad was washing the dishes.

Bits hung up her jacket.

"There's soup on the stove," added Mom, pointing with a half-dried plate.

"I'm not hungry," mumbled Bits. She ran to her room and threw herself on the bed.

A few minutes later, there was a knock on her door. "Bits?" She didn't answer. The door opened and Dad came in carrying a tray with a bowl of soup and a glass of milk on it.

"You'll probably be hungry in a little bit," he said, setting the tray on the floor. He sat on the edge of the bed near her. "Chris told Mom you've been taming a deer. Is it true?"

Bits didn't answer. She didn't care what Chris had told them.

"That explains the run on apples, doesn't it?"

"He just showed up one day. I didn't have anybody at school. I didn't think it would hurt anything." The words came rushing out. Tears stung her eyelids. "Chris hunts. Her whole family hunts!"

"You know," said Dad, "there are hunters and there are hunters. Some could care less about the animal, but many are responsible sportsmen. Then there are those who hunt to help them get through the winter."

"She killed a rabbit," said Bits, "and it wasn't for food."

"Did she say why?"

"She said something about their garden."

"Animals can be destructive sometimes."

Bits chewed the inside of her lip. How could that make killing all right? Wasn't there another way?

"Honey." He touched her knee. "I think the Howards hunt to supplement their income."

What did money have to do with anything? You didn't shoot animals. Period. And why was Dad taking Chris's side? It sounded like he thought it was okay that the Howards hunted.

"My dad and brothers hunted," he said slowly. "Still do."

Bits tensed.

"I remember I couldn't wait to turn twelve so that I could go hunting with them."

"Did you—shoot anything?" Bits held her breath.

"No," answered Dad.

Bits relaxed.

"I had the deer in my gun sight. My hands shook. My heart raced." He paused. "I couldn't bring myself to pull the trigger. My brothers teased me so bad that I tried again the next year. The same thing happened. After that I stopped going." He looked at his hands, then looked at her. "What are you going to do?"

"Wh-what do you mean?" Bits knew what was coming.

"The deer, how are you going to protect him?"

Bits wound a loose pillowcase thread around her forefinger. All afternoon she'd asked herself the same question. There weren't a lot of answers. "I'm going to tear down the deer stand. Then I'm going to build a pen to keep Buck in during hunting season."

She pulled the thread free and rolled it between her fingers, then sat up, waiting for Dad to say something.

"Neither the stand nor the deer are yours," he said finally.

Bits couldn't believe what she was hearing.

"The stand isn't on our property. Whoever built it may need the venison as much as the Howards. As for putting the deer in a pen, that won't solve the real problem, Bits. He isn't afraid of humans anymore."

"He was scared of Chris," said Bits.

"Did he run or try to hide when he saw her?"

"No." She sank deeper into the pillow.

"Honey, you can't keep him locked up. He's still a wild animal. I know you want to help him, but anything you do now will only make it worse. Just leave him alone. Maybe he'll be okay."

This wasn't the way things were supposed to turn out.

"Do you understand what I'm saying?" asked Dad.

"What? Yeah. Sure." There had to be a way to keep Buck safe.

"We can talk more later," said Dad, standing up. "Now why don't you try to eat something." He picked up the tray of food and set it on her lap, then kissed the top of her head and left the room.

Bits stared at the soup. How could she possibly eat? She'd just driven away one friend, and now she might lose Buck, too. There had to be some way around this. She just had to think of it, that's all.

It was almost 10:30 when Bits woke up the next morning. She'd spent most of the night lying awake

trying to come up with a plan. Around 2:30 she had an idea. She went over it and over it, and finally fell asleep.

"Good morning," said Mom when Bits came into the kitchen.

Bits didn't think it felt like such a good morning. "How come it's so bright out?" She squinted.

"It snowed last night."

"It did?" Bits walked over to the window. She hadn't opened the curtains in her room. An inch of snow covered the ground. Even the pine boughs had a white coating. Only one thing disturbed the scene. A fresh set of car tracks scarred the snow in the driveway. Dad must be working this Saturday again.

"Chris was pretty upset when she came back here last night," said Mom. "What happened between you two?"

Bits opened the refrigerator and took out the milk. She hadn't touched any of the food on the tray.

"Bits?"

"I made a big deal out of something she did." Why did Mom have to ask all these questions?

"What did you say to her?"

Bits hesitated. "I—I said she liked killing things."

Mom's stunned silence made Bits feel worse. She hadn't meant to be cruel, but Chris being able to shoot animals didn't make any sense to her.

"You know," said Mom, "when I worked at the

hospital, I learned that you should never put off an apology. I saw a lot of people who let it go until it was too late."

Bits frowned. What did the hospital and dying people have to do with anything? It wasn't like she wouldn't see Chris again. She felt her mother's eyes on her. "I'll call Chris later."

Actually, in a way, she felt grateful to Chris. If she hadn't told her about hunting season, she wouldn't have known about Buck's danger until it was too late. She chewed her lower lip. Yes, she *would* apologize for calling Chris a murderer. But what if Chris asked if they were still friends? Bits didn't know if she could be best friends with someone who hunted.

"I want you to go into town with me later this morning," said Mom. "I need you to watch Jason while we're in the grocery store."

Good, thought Bits. There was still time to work on the deer stand. She dressed and tiptoed back to the kitchen. Mom was in the laundry room. Bits quickly dug the hammer out of the junk drawer and hurried to put on her jacket and boots.

It was warmer outside than she'd thought it would be. There were animal tracks everywhere in the new snow. Some crisscrossed the trail, others ran alongside of it. One track showed two tiny foot marks in front and two in back and a straight line in between. Wherever the feet went, so did the line.

Bits broke into a run. If a little mouse left such a clear trail, hunters would have no problem tracking a deer.

Bits was out of breath when she reached the deer stand. Each rung of the ladder had a thin frosting of snow on it. Bits focused on the bottom board and drew the hammer back, then hesitated in mid-swing. Dad would be angry when he found out what she had done. But how could she leave it here, knowing that Buck was in danger? She'd taught him to come here. No. She had to destroy it! She would take whatever punishment Dad handed out.

Bits slammed the hammer against the wooden step. Snow crystals flew into the air. On the second strike, she heard the nails creak. Each time her hammer crashed into the boards, she felt a little better. Bits stopped to catch her breath. Sweat ran down her neck. She shrugged off her jacket and started in on the third ladder rung. Whoever built this had done a good job. The passing seasons hadn't weakened the ladder at all.

The fourth board dropped to the ground. She couldn't reach the fifth step and the seat. Seizing the left support post, Bits twisted it until the rope squeaked and the platform boards groaned under the pressure. Finally two floor planks popped out of place and tumbled to the ground.

Bits grabbed the other support and worried it until only the rope remained dangling against the

birch's white bark. She collapsed against the tree trunk, panting. Why didn't seeing the ruined deer stand scattered on the ground satisfy her? She had to get rid of those boards. There wasn't time now, but she would come back later and carry the broken platform into the swamp. There it would rot away to nothing.

Bits stared blankly out the car window on the way back from the grocery store. Several trees had bright new orange signs on them. She didn't remember seeing them before. No Hunting—No Trespassing was printed in bold black lettering on each of them. There were other words underneath, but they were too small to read.

"We need to get some of those," said Bits.

"What?"

"Those signs." She pointed to the trees.

Mom looked out Bits's window. "You mean the No Hunting signs? I agree. Next weekend we'll stop at the hardware store and get a few for you to put up."

They'd get more than a few, Bits vowed silently. She was going to plaster those signs everywhere. Even if she had to use all her money to buy them.

Bits helped put groceries away, then slipped away to her bedroom to stuff her pockets with Buck's food. She'd need more food than usual for what she planned to do.

She had it all worked out. First, she'd coax Buck past the iron pipe into the swamp on their property. Next she'd find a safe, protected spot where she could leave food. Until he was used to coming to their new place, she would hide by the deer stand, and if he came around, she would scare him.

Bits reached the ruined deer stand and settled down to wait. She crossed her fingers and squeezed her eyes shut. After deer season was over, they'd meet at their new spot in the swamp. Buddies just like before. They'd take those walks she had day-dreamed about. Maybe next spring when it was warmer, they'd lie on a bed of sweet fern together— she with her head and shoulders resting upon his chest—and bask in the warm sunshine.

Bits opened her eyes, and there was Buck standing ten feet away, studying her.

"I suppose you're wondering about yesterday." Buck lowered his head. "I hope that's a yes," said Bits. She took a deep breath. "All I could see was you hanging from one of those meat hooks, and it would be all my fault." She shuddered. "Chris scared me. But now we know about hunting, and we know what to do, right?" She pulled a carrot out of her pocket and held it in front of her. "Come on."

Buck's nostrils flared. He took a tentative step toward the tempting scent, then another one.

"That's it."

After he finished the carrot, Bits pulled out the

corn. She let Buck smell it, then slowly backed toward the pipe. He followed her. Every few steps she let him have a few kernels. Closer and closer they came to the iron pipe. Soon the corn was gone and she cut up the apple. Bits saw the pipe out of the corner of her eye as she fed Buck the last quarter of apple.

"Don't worry, we'll make it through the hunting season." She wished she felt as confident as she sounded.

14

D ad drove Bits to school Monday morning on his way to the paper company headquarters in Green Bay. The company was putting in a new inventory and payroll computer system, and he was going to learn it.

She was glad for the ride. Her right shoulder and arm were sore and stiff from all the hammering and carrying she'd done over the weekend. She'd spent a good part of Sunday in the swamp. It had taken several trips to hide all the boards in the thick-growing vegetation. And she'd had to search for a spot for Buck. It had been difficult finding her way through the crowded river birch, past leafless red dogwood, and through slimy bogs. But there in the middle of the swamp she had found it—a small moss-covered clearing. It was perfect! Even with the leaves off the trees, she was sure Buck wouldn't be spotted. Now all she had to do was teach him to come there.

"I hope you're not still angry with Chris," said Dad, breaking into her thoughts.

"No," said Bits. She wasn't angry, just confused. Chris had gone on and on about deer hunting when she'd called. She'd told Bits that without hunting season a lot of deer would starve to death during winter. She'd gone on to describe a deer carcass she'd stumbled across last spring. Bits cringed. Chris had said that every rib showed in its frozen body. Would Bits rather see a deer starve to death than be hunted?

"I'll be back Friday night," said Dad, pulling to a stop in the school parking lot. "Anything special you want me to pick up while I'm in Green Bay?"

Bits thought for a moment. "No Hunting—No Trespassing signs." Would he buy them?

"Good idea. Anything else?"

"No." A school bus pulled up behind them. "I'd better go." She swung out the door before he could reach over and give her a hug. He'd let her put up signs, but not build a pen. It didn't make any sense. The tires crunched gravel as the car pulled away.

Bits opened the school door. Chris was waiting for her on the steps to the second floor.

"I'm not the only girl that hunts," said Chris, her chin up. "Half the people in my firearms safety class were female."

Bits managed a small, fleeting smile. "I'm sorry about some of the things I said Friday."

Chris looked surprised. Then she hurried down the steps to Bits. "I didn't realize you knew so little about hunting. I thought for sure you would have heard a gun or two going off near your place. Small game season started the last week of September."

Bits shook her head. How could she have been so naive? "I thought those popping sounds were cars backfiring."

"Really?"

"I'm from Chicago, remember?" Bits studied Chris. Were they still friends? "City kids can be pretty dumb about some things." She cracked a real smile.

An answering grin appeared on Chris's face, then just as suddenly disappeared. She leaned closer. "Don't say anything about the rabbit to my brother Larry or to my mom and dad, okay?"

Bits was puzzled. "Why?"

"Jeremy and I told them he got it."

"Oh." Bits was going to ask if her parents didn't want her to go hunting when Travis bumped into her. He wore a bright orange cap and a black and orange jacket.

"It's started," said Chris. She nodded toward Travis and the bus load of kids coming in the door.

"What's started?"

"The blaze-orange fashion show," answered Chris.

Bits looked at her. "The what?"

"Blaze-orange is the color all the deer hunters wear so we don't shoot each other," explained Chris. "My grandfather used to call it 'the red wave.' They used to wear red clothing. Some of the guys start wearing their caps in September. But around Halloween everything comes out—jackets, vests, even pants. Mom says it's the only time men like to go shopping. We get Thanksgiving week off from school just for hunting."

Bits had seen the caps, but hadn't realized what they meant. "Don't the deer see them?" Two more kids with orange caps passed her. Then a high-school boy walked by wearing an orange jacket.

"No," answered Chris. "They can only see in black and white."

Too bad, thought Bits. If deer could see that orange, boy, would they run for their lives!

Chris glanced at the clock. "We'd better get going."

Bits followed Chris down the hall. She still didn't understand wanting to hunt. Maybe it would help if she thought about the woods as a big outdoor supermarket, only instead of plopping things in the grocery cart, you had to shoot them. No packaging; no standing in long checkout lines. The bell rang and Bits hurried to her classroom.

Fifteen minutes later Jeremy passed Bits a note. "Heard about your deer. That's really cool." was scribbled on a ripped piece of lined paper.

Bits's heart sank. Jeremy knew about Buck. That meant Chris had broken her promise. "Who else knows?" She scribbled on the back of his note, and slid it between the nape of his neck and his shirt collar.

Jeremy pretended to stretch his arms behind his head. He crumpled the note into his fist as he pulled his arms back down.

Bits couldn't wait for him to write an answer. "Well?" she whispered.

"Nobody," answered Jeremy when Mrs. Carlson turned to write on the blackboard.

"Did Chris tell you?"

"She didn't," answered Jeremy. "I overheard her on the phone when she was talking to you."

Bits was relieved. Chris hadn't broken her promise after all. But what about Jeremy? "You won't tell anyone, will you?"

"Elizabeth," snapped Mrs. Carlson. "Perhaps you'd like to let the rest of the class in on your secret."

Bits felt her face turning red. She shook her head no. Two seats ahead and one row over, Julie turned around to smirk at her. Some day, Julie was going to get into trouble or be embarrassed, and Bits hoped she'd be around to see it!

Jeremy raised his hand to scratch his shoulder. A note dropped from his fingers onto her desk.

"Don't worry, I'll keep your secret." was written on it in pen.

It rained all afternoon. Bits put food out near the swamp, but didn't wait. The next day was clear, and she made Buck follow her to the edge of the marsh before she gave him any food. He complained as he followed her—his voice more insistent with each step. A couple of times he butted her arm with his muzzle.

"Don't be so pushy," said Bits. She stopped when they reached the line of river birch. As he nibbled the corn kernels in her hand, she stroked his soft fur from cheek to shoulder. His neck was bigger, she was sure of it. Was it possible? And why was he so demanding all of a sudden?

Suddenly, he nipped her hand.

"Ouch!" She yanked her hand away. The bite had surprised more than hurt her. She shook her finger at him and opened her mouth to scold him. Gently, he licked her forefinger. This was maddening! He was acting like Jason, pestering her one minute, sweet the next.

She turned back to the swamp. "Well, come on," she said. He stayed where he was. She pulled an apple slice out of her pocket. "If you want this, you have to come and get it."

His nose quivered. How gracefully he threaded

his way around the river birch! When he reached her, she let him have the apple wedge as a reward. Then she continued deeper into the swamp. He didn't follow.

"Come on. It's not much farther." She wouldn't give him the rest until they reached the new spot.

Buck just stared at her. The new location must be making him nervous. "It's for your own good," she coaxed. But Buck turned and melted into the woods, back the way they had come.

"Buck? Buck? Come back here!" Bits tried to run after him, but her foot slipped into a bog hole. The marshy water was ice cold.

What was going on? He had run away as if there was something he *had* to do, and he had to do it right now.

At least they'd almost made it to their new place. Tomorrow he would follow her all the way.

Friday morning Bits walked into the girls' bathroom. Julie and Karen were standing in front of one of the sinks. As Bits walked by them, Julie pulled Karen away in mock terror.

"Careful," said Julie. "She might want to poke a hole in your ear."

Bits swallowed her retort. What good would it do to tell them what jerks they were? Besides, two against one was lousy odds. She fumed in the stall

until they were gone. Coward! she thought, banging the stall door with a vengeance.

On the metal ledge below the mirror where Julie and Karen had stood was a wrapped tampon. One of them must have her period. Bits had started hers last summer. She remembered how embarrassed she'd been when Kersten had teased her about it in front of Shanti.

A slow grin spread across her face. Bits laughed. "If only I have the guts to pull it off." She tore the wrapper off the tampon, pulled it from its protective cardboard covering, and wrapped the exposed tampon in paper towels. She smiled at herself in the mirror. Then she slowly stuck her head out around the bathroom door. Now where were those two?

Julie was halfway down the hall standing in front of her locker. Karen was there, too, peering over Julie's shoulder at something. Please God, Bits prayed, don't let them turn around. She eased out of the bathroom, dodging to keep the other kids in the hall between her and Julie. It was perfect. Everyone would see the tampon on the floor behind Julie. Two more steps. Could she really do it? Her hands were clammy. She was there. . . .

Bits passed the girls, head down, eyes glued to the floor. When she reached the end of the hall, she slid into the corner and leaned against the cool gray

metal of the lockers. She couldn't do it. It was too mean—even for someone like Julie.

"What's with the paper towels?" Chris was standing in front of her.

"Ah—I was going to wipe out my locker," lied Bits.

Someone screamed back down the hall.

Bits jumped. "What happened?"

"Travis tossed a walking-stick into Julie's locker."

"You mean a cane? I don't get it. What for?"

"No, Bits, it's an insect that's about three inches long."

"Yuck!" Bits shivered. A frenzied Julie was slamming her notebook again and again against the locker door. So much for the walking-stick.

The bell went off.

Well, thought Bits, all good things come to an end. She dropped the crushed toweling into a trash can on her way to class.

Bits sat with Chris at lunch. Kids were still talking about the walking-stick incident. Jeremy and Travis sat two tables away. Julie and Karen were nowhere in sight.

"What are you doing about your deer?" asked Chris, scraping the tomato sauce off her pizza slice.

"I'm moving him into our swamp," answered

Bits. "He followed me part of the way on Tuesday. But Wednesday he wouldn't come to me, and last night he didn't show up at all. I'm getting worried."

"My dad says rutting season has started. Maybe he's got a girlfriend, and that's why he isn't showing up," said Chris. "Last year it peaked the week before hunting season opened."

"Oh." At least it wasn't something dangerous. "Would that make him act weird or make his neck bigger?"

"Un-huh, bucks get bigger necks during rut," answered Chris. She looked at Bits. "How did he act?"

"Kind of demanding, and not interested in food."

Chris thought about it. "All I know is that my dad says bucks have just one thing on their minds during rut, and that's finding a doe." She giggled. "Sounds like my older brother." She leaned across the table and lowered her voice. "Sometimes I hear Larry talking about girls to Jeremy."

Bits barely heard the last sentence. She knew it was silly to feel jealous, but she couldn't help it.

Just then Jeremy came by. "Look." He showed Chris a picture. "Travis's brother got him by the river last weekend." Travis came up behind him.

"One, two, three . . . eight points!" Chris seemed impressed.

"Yep," beamed Travis. "Weighed over two hundred pounds, too."

Bits snatched the picture from Chris. A smiling boy who looked like an older Travis held a deer by the antlers. She swallowed. "Is he dead?"

"No-o," drawled Travis. "My brother wrestled it to the ground." He gave her a "what-planet-do-you-come-from" look. "Of course it's dead."

Bits couldn't believe it. "B-but it isn't deer season yet."

"It is for archers," answered Travis. He took his picture off to show someone else.

Bits wheeled on Chris. "Why didn't you tell me! When did it start?"

"Oh, Bits, I forgot," moaned Chris. "It goes until a week before gun season, then starts up again afterward and goes till the end of December. Don't look at me like that. I'm sorry, I didn't think of it. I don't know anybody who hunts with a bow."

A terrible thought stole into Bits's mind. "Maybe that's why Buck didn't show up last night."

"Bits, there aren't that many bow hunters."

"How many?" she shot back.

"I don't know the exact number!"

Bits's mind raced. "Oh, no!" All the color drained from her cheeks.

"What's wrong?"

"A couple of weekends ago I saw two guys across the road from our place. They were driving four-wheelers and had gray cases strapped to the racks behind the drivers' seats."

"Probably bow cases," said Chris.

Bits panicked. What if they came back? Maybe they had been back. She could almost see the snapshot of Buck, his limp head held by a grinning hunter. She jumped up, forgetting her tray.

"Where are you going?" asked Chris.

"Home."

Chris caught her arm. "Wait! How are you going to get home?"

"I'll call my mom and tell her I'm sick."

"She won't let you out of the house then."

Chris was right. If she said she was sick, Mom would put her to bed. Would Mom let her out if she told the truth? No. She had to stay in school. Bits looked at the lunchroom clock. Three more hours. They were going to be the longest three hours of her life.

15

Bits squirmed through the endless bus ride home. She tore down their driveway and into the house, dropped her backpack onto the table, and yanked open the junk drawer.

"Bits, what's the matter?" asked Mom.

"I have to scare Buck." She rooted through the drawer. Where was the hammer?

"Bits, slow down. Now stop."

Not now, Bits pleaded silently. I don't have time for a lecture now.

"What are you looking for?"

"The hammer." Why wasn't it here?

"It's in the laundry room. I was using it to put up—"

Bits whipped down the hallway.

"It's by the washing machine," called Mom.

Clutching the hammer, Bits ran out through the kitchen. She pulled the lid off the metal garbage can by the back door, then dashed headlong down the

trail. How was she going to find Buck? She'd waited by the river birch for the past two days, but he hadn't come to her. The clearing. That's where he'd be!

The birch tree looked naked without the deer stand. Bits leaned against the scarred white trunk to catch her breath. She half wished the stand was still there so she could climb up to get a better view of the area.

She scanned the edges of the clearing carefully. Her ears strained for any sound that might mean Buck was nearby. "Please show up." Her words sounded so small in all that open space. Her hands were cramping from clutching the hammer and garbage can lid so tightly.

The shadow cast by the pine trees near the fallen log stretched longer and longer, but still there was no sign of Buck. Bits wished she'd thought to bring an apple along to lure him to her. Tomorrow, she promised herself. It would be risky drawing him back to this spot, but she didn't have much choice now.

Dusk settled over the clearing. The temperature dropped. Bits shivered. Even the chickadees and red squirrels were quiet. Bits stumbled through the dark back to the house. But she'd be back: tomorrow and the next day and the next. No matter how long it took, she'd keep coming—for Buck.

* * *

"Oh, I bought those signs you asked for," said Dad between mouthfuls of bacon and egg. He had come home late last night from Green Bay. Bits picked up a bag that was leaning against the wall and tipped it upside down next to her plate. Three plastic-wrapped packages of bright orange signs and a roll of inch-wide ribbon slid onto the table. There were ten signs to a package. "What's the ribbon for?"

"To tie the signs to the trees," Dad answered. He took a sip of coffee. "Didn't you understand what I was trying to tell you last week? I hoped you'd leave that deer alone so he could get some of his natural wariness back, but Mom tells me you're still seeing him." He put down his cup. "How many times have you seen him this week?"

"Twice," she answered, "but only one counts. I only saw him for a few seconds Wednesday—he didn't even come near me."

Dad took another sip of coffee. "Mom told me you're trying to scare him."

Bits wasn't sure if this was a question or a state-ment, but she answered anyway. "Chris told me it's bow season now, and I think I saw a couple of hunters across the road."

"Ah, I forgot about bow hunting."

"So did Chris." Chris had called the night before to say she'd forgotten to warn Bits that there were

poachers in the area. Bits hoped she hadn't forgotten anything else.

"I hope it works," said Dad.

"Me, too," said Bits.

After breakfast, Bits headed down the driveway with scissors, ribbon, and signs. Her breath made white puffs in the cold air. She pushed the collar of her winter coat up and pulled her cap down over her ears.

Fallen leaves carpeted the driveway. The leaves were covered with fuzzy white frost. She wanted to stop and touch them, but there wasn't time.

An engine rumbled in the distance. As she got closer to the road, the sound got louder. A four-wheeler? No. A brown pickup rolled slowly past the entrance to their driveway. The driver was leaning out the window, looking at the ground. He wore an orange cap.

Bits ran toward the road. The truck was driving down the wrong side of the road. What was that guy doing anyway? Bits wondered as the pickup disappeared around a curve.

Bits followed the truck, scanning the shoulder where the driver had been looking. She soon saw what the man had been staring at—fresh deer tracks. Were they Buck's? No. A second, smaller set of tracks followed the larger ones. It had to be a doe and her fawn.

Bits tracked the prints across the road to the other side. They led to a definite trail in the brush. A deer trail! She wondered how many hunters knew it was here.

A quarter-mile down the trail, it intersected with the logging road she and Jason had explored the day she'd seen the bow hunters. The four-wheeler tracks were still faintly visible in the sand, but there were no fresh tracks. The hunters hadn't been back since she'd seen them then. But that didn't mean they wouldn't come back this weekend. That pickup had been scouting for signs of deer; there must be others like him. And all she could do was put up these dumb signs.

A dead white pine lay off to her right. Bits dragged a rotten ten-foot section of it out of the grass and across the path, then scoured the area for more deadfall. Slowly she built up a respectable road-block. She tied a No Hunting sign to a branch. Nobody would get by that!

She built another roadblock on the path that lead to Buck's clearing. The property belonged to the paper company, but Bits didn't care. Besides, she'd never seen any paper company people out here any-way. They'd never know the difference.

Then she put signs up and down the path every hundred feet. She saved the last for the red pine in their clearing.

* * *

After lunch, Bits headed back to the woods with her hammer and garbage-can lid. This time she made sure to bring an apple along. When she reached the white birch, she sliced the fruit and rubbed the halves against the bark. Then she set the hammer and lid on the ground and scrunched down to wait. Two ravens flew overhead. "A-w-k, you won't see him, a-w-k, you won't see him," they seemed to call.

Bits bit her lip. "He'll show up. I know he will." She ripped a piece of bark from the birch tree, peeled off a thin strip, and let it drop to the ground. A pile of white curls began to grow at her feet. When there was nothing left of the piece of bark, she started to pace.

"Come on, Buck," she muttered. "Let's get this over with." Maybe singing would help. It was the last thing she felt like doing, but it had worked before. She forced herself. "O Christmas tree, O Christmas tree . . ."

The time dragged by. Bits couldn't keep this up much longer. Her throat was desert dry. Then, at last, she heard a twig snap. She whipped her head around toward the sound. "Please be Buck."

It was! He paused to check the air.

What a relief! Buck was okay—for now. Bits steeled herself. She hated what she had to do. She picked up the hammer and lid.

Buck ambled toward her. His black nose quivered

at the scent of apple; his brown eyes were so trusting. Why was he making this so hard?

"You know I promised that I'd always be your
friend, that I would never hurt you. Remember?"

He stopped and cocked his head at her voice.

Her voice broke. "I'm going to keep my promise,
Buck." She choked back tears. The muscles in her
arms and shoulders tensed. She raised the hammer
and lid above her head and crashed them together.
"Go!" she shouted and continued crashing. "Get
out of here!"

Buck leaped into the trees, then stopped, quivering with indecision.

Bits followed him, slamming the hammer against
the lid. "Didn't you hear me? I'm doing this for
your own good!"

He trotted deeper into the brush. She stumbled
after him. Blam! Blam! Blam! Finally she lowered
her aching arms and wiped her tears on her jacket
sleeve.

He was still there—behind some pine boughs,
peering at her.

"Don't you understand?" Bits pleaded. "I mean
it. Get out of here!" She stumbled toward him. Her
lungs burned. Her arms felt like Silly Putty. She
couldn't catch her breath. The lid and hammer
slipped from her sweaty grasp. She dropped to her
knees, panting.

"Why won't you go away?" she croaked. Her hair was full of twigs and needles, and her cheek was scratched. The bitter taste of failure filled her mouth.

Buck inched his way toward her.

"No," Bits said weakly.

He lowered his head until his large eyes were level with hers.

"Go away." Tears streamed down her cheeks.

She could feel his breath on her left cheek. Gently he licked her salty tears. She reached up and buried her face in his neck. "What are we going to do?"

"He won't scare." Bits slumped into a kitchen chair.

Her parents were silent. The only sound came from Jason, who was playing with blocks on the floor.

"You need to hurt him in some way," said Mom finally.

"Hurt him?" She couldn't do that.

"Bits, do you remember? You must have been three. You loved to play with the knobs on the stove. Your dad and I tried everything, but you wouldn't leave them alone—until you burned your arm. Remember? We had to take you to the emergency room, but you never touched that stove again. Sometimes pain can teach when nothing else can."

Bits rubbed the scar on her arm. How could she cause Buck pain? Could she hurt him on purpose? "I suppose I could throw pinecones at him."

"I have an idea," said Dad. "Come on."

Bits followed him out to the garage. She watched him pull the inner tube out of his bike tire.

"I don't think we'll be biking any more this year." He cut a ten-inch-long strip of rubber off the inner tube, then he led her into the trees next to the garage. He sawed off a Y-shaped branch. "This will work." Dad rounded the rough ends with his jack-knife and tied the strip of rubber to the points.

"Hey, neat!" said Bits.

Her dad smiled. "Everybody had a slingshot when I was a kid."

She raised an eyebrow. "Does it work?"

"If you practice. I used to be pretty good with one of these." He looked around. "There aren't a lot of small rocks up here, so we'll use pinecones." He unfolded a moving box and began filling it. "There's your target." He pointed to the young aspen tree by the drive. "Give it a try. Like this."

Dad put a pinecone against the rubber, then pulled back the sling. Zing. The first cone flew past the tree. "Like I said, I *used* to be pretty good." He tried again. This time the cone hit the tree squarely. "Here, you try it."

Bits's thumb slipped and the cone flipped into the air, landing four feet away. She tried again. The cone

flew past the tree. The next time she hit the trunk.

"Now you're getting it." He handed her a pine-cone and she reloaded.

Blat! The cone bounced off the target.

"All *right*," said Dad.

Bits smiled. This might work after all. After three more cones hit their mark, she backed up ten feet. Could she still hit the target from farther away?

Daylight was fading, so Dad went into the house to turn on the yard light. She practiced until Mom called them in for dinner. "We'll have to start calling you Eagle-Eyed Elizabeth." Dad grinned as they headed in.

"Geeze, Dad!" Bits grinned back. This *had* to be the answer.

16

The next afternoon Bits straddled the fallen tree where she had first laid apples to attract Buck. Her backpack was slung over her shoulder, filled with hard cones from a Norway pine. Her hands were sticky from rubbing an apple on a nearby tree. She spat on her palms and tried to rub some of the stickiness onto her jeans. She didn't want anything to ruin her aim. Bits frowned. Hunters probably thought that, too.

She wasn't sure it was him at first. Then she saw the antlers.

"Buck," she called.

His big ears angled toward her.

She rose and walked toward him, fitting the first pinecone into her sling. Where should she aim? Did he have a tender spot somewhere? She drew back the rubber and fired.

The cone bounced off his forehead. Buck leapt

back. Bits thought he looked confused. She reloaded quickly and shot him again.

This one hit his shoulder. He sidestepped as she fired, and the cone fell onto the needle-covered ground behind him. Buck's left ear swiveled toward where it landed. Her fourth shot ricocheted off his rump, but he just looked annoyed, not frightened.

She had to hit him harder. Pulling the rubber back as far as she could, Bits let him have it full in the face. The cone hit him on the cheek. He spun around. Good. She'd finally found a tender spot! Now if she could just keep the pressure on.

Bits chased Buck around the clearing, firing as she ran. He danced ahead of her as if he thought she was playing! Bits was angry now. Only a few cones remained in her bag. She fired in quick succession. Three of them hit their mark, the fourth bounced off a tree branch. Buck stood there switching his tail. Was he laughing at her?

She reached into her bag for more ammunition, but came up empty. Now what was she going to do? Buck lowered his head to nibble on a nearby plant. Furious, Bits hurled the slingshot at him. It bounced off his rump. "Go on!" she yelled. "Get out of here!" She grabbed whatever she could get her hands on—branches, sticks, pieces of bark—and flung them at him. Everything fell short. Buck trotted easily out of her range, then turned to see if she was still playing the game.

She stopped, panting. It was useless. She would have to come up with another plan.

"It was a good try," said Dad as he drove Bits to school Monday morning. Bits didn't say anything.

Dad was on his way to Green Bay again. "There are still twelve days before gun season opens," he continued. "Stay away from him. That might be enough time for him to forget you."

Bits stared out the window. If only she could be sure. She'd gotten him into this mess. It was up to her to keep him safe. The car pulled into the parking lot, and Bits hopped out.

She found Chris waiting for her by her locker. "My mom says you can tell how much money people have by how many new hunting clothes they buy."

Bits inspected her classmates. The number of orange-clad boys had doubled from last week. She sighed. "Buck won't scare. I've tried everything. But he keeps coming back."

"Why don't you build a fence?" suggested Chris.

"What about the poachers and bow hunters you told me about?"

"What about them?" asked Chris.

Bits shook her head. "You told me bow hunting goes till the end of December. I couldn't keep Buck penned up that long."

"There aren't that many bow hunters. The colder

it gets, the fewer there are. And the poachers aren't going to hunt by your house. They'll drive down some lumber trail where they won't be seen."

Bits thought it over. Maybe a fence would work. But Dad had already said no. If she told him what Chris had just told her, would he understand? It would only be for sixteen days.

Bits chewed the inside of her lip. How was she going to build a fence? "The old outhouse boards!"

"What?" asked Chris.

"We've got a pile of lumber from an old outhouse someone tore down. I could use the boards to build a fence."

"Where?" asked Chris.

"I'm not sure," answered Bits. Buck probably wouldn't follow her all the way home, so she couldn't put it too close to the house. "Maybe somewhere near the swamp." She squeezed Chris's arm. "How big would it have to be?"

Chris shrugged. "I don't know."

"Take a guess," insisted Bits.

Chris looked around. "Maybe as wide as this hall and as long as from here to Mrs. Carlson's door."

Bits put one foot in front of the other, heel to toe, heel to toe.

"What are you doing?" asked Chris.

"Measuring." She'd seen Mom do this at home. She reached the lockers on the other side and turned toward Mrs. Carlson's door. She was con-

centrating so hard on the distance she didn't even notice the strange looks from her classmates. "It's ten feet wide by twelve feet long," she called to Chris when she reached Mrs. Carlson's door. "Can you come over tomorrow night?"

Chris joined her. "Mom doesn't work, but it's a school night," she said. "She'll probably say no, but I'll ask anyway."

"Good," said Bits.

Bits braced herself as she entered the kitchen. All day she'd practiced her speech about why she should build a fence. "I'm going to build a pen for Buck," she announced. "It's the only thing left to do. Chris thinks it's a good idea. I know Dad doesn't like it, but he's wrong. . . . "

"You don't have to convince me," said Mom, raising her hand. "I agree with you."

"You do?"

"Yes," answered Mom. "As a matter of fact, I talked to your dad about it last night. He isn't crazy about the idea, but I think he realizes it's the only option left."

Bits sauntered out of the house. She hadn't felt this good in days. Mom had even said she could have all the food she needed to attract Buck to his new home. But first Bits had to decide where to build the pen.

She walked down the trail, searching the terrain

for the perfect spot. There were too many trees up here. She ducked under some low pine boughs and veered left toward the swamp by the lake. Fifty feet from the marsh, she found the place. Jack pines made natural barriers along two sides of a small clearing. A white pine and a couple of pointy balsam firs formed the third side. She'd have to fill in the gaps, of course, then build some kind of gate on the fourth side. First she'd need to cut and haul some branches out of the way, though.

She found a saw in the garage, stuffed her pockets with food and returned to the woods.

The trail to the red pine wound down the slope, less than five hundred feet from Buck's new home. Bits could just see the fluttering orange ribbon on the property marker through the jack pines. She'd lure Buck with food, just like she'd coaxed him to the deer stand. She'd lay a trail of food from the iron pipe toward the swamp. Each day she would move Buck closer and closer to the pen.

By Tuesday, Bits had cleared the brush and trimmed the trees in the jack pine clearing. It was hard work. She wished Chris could have come home with her. Then the work would've been easier, even fun. At least she was coming on Friday night.

The next day Bits carried the old outhouse boards to the pen. More gray splinters dotted her clothes after each load. On Thursday she finished transport-

ing the wood and even had time to pound a few of the boards into the trees before darkness fell, then she had to quit.

The sky was a dark gray as Bits walked up the driveway on Friday morning. It looked like rain or even snow. She hoped it wasn't snow. Bits smiled to herself; soon it wouldn't matter anymore. Buck would be safe in his pen, and it could snow all it wanted.

At 11:30, Mr. Grant made an announcement over the public address system. "Rain changing to freezing rain is expected this afternoon, making travel hazardous. Buses will be leaving at noon to take students home."

"All right!" whispered Bits and smiled. Now she and Chris would have more time to work on the fence.

At 11:55, the students were released from their classrooms. Bits and Chris hurried for the bus. Bits slipped on the icy sidewalk and would have fallen if Chris hadn't caught her.

The bus looked like something out of an old horror movie. Its sides were coated with dirty, half-melted ice.

"Do you get a lot of snow days up here?" asked Bits.

"No," answered Chris. "Only when we get freezing rain or tons of snow."

The blacktopped roads were covered with ice,

and the bus crawled over them. Only when they turned on to a sandy road did the driver dare accelerate. Bits wondered if her dad would make it home tonight.

By the time Bits and Chris jumped off the bus, the freezing sleet had let up a little. But the twigs on the trees along the driveway were twice their normal size because of their coatings of ice.

"I think you'd better wait until tomorrow to work on Buck's pen," said Mom when they entered the house. "You'll just get soaked out there."

Bits dropped her pack. There wasn't time to wait. She had to finish building the pen this weekend. She needed next week to coax Buck into it.

"Your dad called," said Mom. "It's even worse east of here. He's going to spend the weekend in Green Bay."

"I know what we can do," said Bits. She opened the cupboard below the sink and took out two large garbage bags. "We can wear these over our coats. That way we'll stay dry, just like the street people back home."

Chris looked surprised. "Wear a garbage bag?"

"Sure," said Bits. She cut a hole in the bottom seam for her head, then one on each side for her arms. Then she slipped the bag over her head. "See?" She turned around, modeling for her mom and Chris.

"Well, I suppose you'll be all right," said Mom.

"But I want you back in this house as soon as you get cold. Do you hear me?"

"I promise," said Bits, handing Chris a bag.

When they neared the pen, Bits put food out, but it was immediately encased in ice. Would Buck eat frozen vegetables? She glanced around, then took a couple of boughs and made a lean-to over the food. She knew Buck would know it was there. He'd eaten every pile she'd left this week, and today's new pile was only fifty feet from the pen.

"I brought the nails you asked for," said Chris.

Bits peeked into the ice-crusted paper bag. These nails were longer than the ones she'd been using.

"I think you're going to run out of boards," said Chris. The pile of outhouse wood did look inadequate compared to the size of the clearing. Geometry wasn't Bits's strong suit. "We could use the deer stand. I tore it down and dumped it over there." Bits pointed with an icy mitten.

"That'll help, but you're still going to run out."

Bits didn't know what else to do. There was no more wood. She could feel the desperation rising in her throat.

"Wait a minute!" cried Chris. "If we leave spaces between the boards, there might be enough."

Bits yanked off every other board from those she'd nailed up the day before, leaving a gap between the boards. "Like this?" Chris nodded.

Bits was glad she'd thought to stash the lumber

well under the white pine. The bushy boughs had kept the wood mostly free of ice. Chris drove the nails through the old boards while Bits held them in place and handed her the nails. After a while they traded places. Bits's arm ached after only two boards. Again they switched. Chris was stronger. She was able to get up three boards before her arm gave out.

When they'd used all the outhouse planks, they waded through the underbrush to the deer-stand boards. It was slow going. River birch branches slashed their plastic-bag coats. The half-frozen ground was treacherous. It started to sleet again, and they kept their heads down to avoid the sharp pellets. It was almost dark when they hauled the last of the deer-stand boards to the pen.

"Bits? Chris?" Mom was calling them. Too tired to talk, they dropped the boards and trudged home.

"That's good," said Chris, swallowing the hot tea that Bits's mom had brewed for them. She took another sip. "What are we going to do for a gate?"

"I don't know," answered Bits.

"Chicken wire might work," suggested Chris.

Bits toweled her damp hair. Chicken wire? How would she get that? Dad could have picked it up for her, but he wouldn't be back in time. She'd have to ask Mom to go into town and buy some.

After dinner, the girls retreated to Bits's bedroom. Bits sneaked back to the kitchen while her

mom was in the laundry room, filled a bowl with ice cubes, then got the rubbing alcohol from the bathroom.

"What's up?" asked Chris, as Bits dumped the booty on her desk.

"I have the stuff to pierce your ear," answered Bits.

Chris cringed when Bits took the needle out of her desk and poured alcohol over it. "Will it hurt?"

"A little," admitted Bits.

"Ah-h, maybe we should wait. I—I don't have any earrings."

"I told you you could have one of mine," said Bits.

"Oh, yeah," Chris answered weakly.

"You'll have to pull your hair back."

Slowly Chris gathered her long hair into a ponytail. Bits leaned over her. The needle glinted in the light from the overhead lamp.

Chris grabbed her wrist. "You won't make more than one hole, will you?"

Bits shook her head. "Don't be scared," she said. "I've done this before. I even did my own second and third holes. See?" She removed the top two earrings and showed Chris the holes. Chris still looked terrified. "I won't do it if you don't want me to."

"I—I do," said Chris. "It's just that I have this . . ." She took a deep breath. "Do it!" Her eyes snapped shut.

A couple of minutes later Bits was wiping the red spot on Chris's earlobe with alcohol.

Chris opened her eyes. "That wasn't so bad. The ice hurt more than the needle. I could hear the needle when you pushed it through, though. It sounded creepy."

Chris held an alcohol-soaked tissue around the hole while Bits poured alcohol over the earring post. "You can't take this out until the hole heals," she instructed. "After a few weeks you can change earrings."

Chris inserted the post and inspected herself in the mirror while Bits screwed the cap back on the alcohol. Chris's reaction to the needle had surprised her. "How can you be so squeamish about getting your ear pierced and not about other things?" she asked.

"What do you mean?" Chris admired her newly pierced ear in the mirror.

"You know—about hunting."

Chris let her hair fall. "I don't know." She paused. "All I know is that I've been scared of needles ever since I was a little kid."

"But you aren't afraid of guns?"

"No. Everyone in our family knows how to handle a gun safely—except for Lisa, of course. But when she turns twelve, she'll go to firearms safety classes just like I did."

Bits was torn. Here was Chris helping her build a

pen for Buck this week, and next week the same girl was going deer hunting.

"Bits, we're not like the slob hunters out there. My dad would have a fit if one of us acted irresponsibly with a gun. Like last year when Larry wounded a buck. He and my dad trailed it for almost three hours to make sure it wouldn't suffer."

"What are slob hunters?"

"Jerks!" Chris stood up. "That's what they are." She pulled down the covers on the rollaway bed. "They shoot at the slightest sound. Without even seeing a deer, they whip around and fire off four or five rounds. And if they hit a deer and it doesn't drop right away, they're too lazy to find out for sure if they wounded it." She plopped down on the bed. "Those are the ones I hate the most. They give the rest of us a bad name."

Bits was shocked. She'd never seen Chris this angry before. She changed into her pajamas and crawled into bed.

"You know that deer carcass I told you I found last spring?"

Bits raised herself up on her elbow. "Yeah?"

"Do you know why he starved to death?" said Chris. "There were so many deer, there wasn't enough food for them all, and the snow was too deep that winter for them to move to another area."

Bits lay back down. The more Chris told her, the more confusing it all was. "Don't they have any

enemies?" she asked. "Like when birds eat bugs?"

"There are a few wolf packs west of here, but not nearly enough to keep the deer numbers down. It's up to us hunters."

Bits reached up and turned out the light. She wished she could go back to the days in the city, when she knew nothing about guns or hunting. She could hear Chris breathing in the quiet darkness. There was still one question she had to ask. Should she ask it now? "Why do you *want* to go hunting?"

"I'm not sure," said Chris finally. "I love listening to my dad when he talks about what it's like out there early in the morning. He says you can hear the world wake up, the rustle of leaves and grass as the squirrels and rabbits begin moving around. He says you can hear a pinecone drop to the ground. And when the sun comes up and you spot the deer, he says their breath comes out in white puffs and surrounds their heads like halos." She paused. "He says when you're out there, you can feel God."

17

oo bad they closed the town dump," said Chris at breakfast the next morning. "I bet we'd have found a gate even better than chicken wire."

"Hey, that's it!" Bits nearly choked on her cereal. "Jason and I were out walking a few weeks ago, and we came across this junk pile. There was an old stuffed chair, a funny-looking bike, a rusty bed-spring—"

"A bedspring! Great!" said Chris "We can use that for a gate."

Bits had a hard time picturing a bedspring as a gate.

"Believe me, it'll work," said Chris. "Come on, let's go."

The jumbled heap was just as Bits had left it.

"We'll have to get some of the other stuff off first," said Chris, climbing the icy pile.

Bits followed, banging her shin painfully on the leg of an ancient-looking washing machine. They pushed off a chair, then a rusted bike frame.

"This is heavy," puffed Bits as they lifted the full-size spring onto its side. They pushed it, end over end, off the pile. It tumbled to the ground, its metal coils vibrating.

"We'll have to take rests carrying it back," said Chris.

It took them an hour to reach Buck's pen. They leaned the bedspring against the trees, then fell panting to the grass.

"This better work," said Bits, massaging her sore hands.

"It should," said Chris. "Now all we need is some rope."

"I think there's some in the garage from when we moved."

The rope hung coiled on the garage wall. The girls paused only to chug a tumbler each of water from the kitchen sink and hurried back to work. Chris bound the steel rim of the bedspring securely to a jack pine. "Now all we have to do is move this side over to that white pine and tie it, and we've got our gate!"

Bits lifted the free end of the spring and dragged it to the tree, then back again. It worked!

At ten o'clock, Mr. Howard came to pick up Chris. She was supposed to baby-sit Lisa at 10:30. Her mom was working the eleven-to-five shift today.

"How are the roads?" asked Bits's mom, shivering in her sweater.

"The dirt roads are fine," answered Mr. Howard from the truck. "I haven't been on any of the paved ones yet." He paused. "Thinking about going into town?"

"Yes, we were."

"I heard on the radio that the sanding crews have been out all night. You shouldn't have any trouble."

"When you're in town, get some chicken wire to wrap around the trees above the boards. Deer can jump pretty high." Chris lowered her voice. "Thanks for the post." Pulling her hair aside she showed Bits her ear. "See you later." The pickup disappeared down the driveway.

There were orange-clad men everywhere: on the sidewalks, in the grocery store, in every pickup truck. At least a dozen trucks were parked in front of the Sportsmen's Shop. Bits cringed. The license plates came from Illinois and Iowa as well as Wisconsin. So many hunters! And they all were after her Buck.

Home at last, Mom and Bits carried the fifty-pound bag of corn into the garage. Bits filled a large metal bowl from the kitchen with the yellow kernels and carried it to the pen. Next she carried down the twenty-five pound apple-flavored mineral lick. Mom had thought of that. And finally she took down a bagful of apples and carrots.

Bits checked the food she'd put out the day

before. Everything was gone. Only fifty feet lay between her and the pen. She placed the new apples and carrots halfway to the gate.

Sunday morning Bits finished the fence. She'd run out of the long nails Chris had brought and gone back to using shorter ones. Mom came down with a stepladder and helped. Together they nailed the chicken wire to the trees. Bits climbed down to the ground and inspected her work. From the ground to the top of the chicken wire, the fence was almost eight feet tall. There was no way Buck could jump out now.

After a quick trip home for lunch, Bits settled herself down by the food pile to wait. She thought that maybe her singing would bring Buck to her, but she gave up on the third chorus of "O Christmas Tree." Time trickled by. She raked a stick back and forth in the sand. Why did Buck have to be in rut? It made so him unpredictable. She was even beginning to wonder if it was Buck who was eating the food. Chris had told her that the older bucks did most of the mating. If that was true, then why wasn't he here with her?

Gunshots sounded in the distance. Bits jerked her head up so fast her neck cracked. It wasn't hunting season yet! Four more shots—then four more. It had to be somebody at target practice. She looked through the trees toward the iron pipe, then she picked an apple from the food pile and rubbed the

pulp on the trees and the boards of the pen. She even rubbed some on the bedspring.

The temperature was dropping as the sunlight began to fade. Bits returned to the food pile and sat down. She could wait just a little longer. The cold seeped into her hands and feet. She ground her stick into the sand. Five more days before hunting season opened. If Buck didn't show up, how was she going to save him? Finally the darkness defeated her, and she stumbled back to the house.

It was snowing when Bits woke up on Monday morning. Large flakes stuck to her clothes as she ran down to the pen. She knew Buck would stay bedded down until the worst of the storm was over, but she wanted to check the food. It was gone! Quickly she made a trail of apples and carrots leading the last few feet into the pen, then raced back to the house to get ready for school.

Tuesday afternoon, the food leading to the pen was gone. The bowl she'd filled with corn was empty, too. She rubbed more apple on the boards and trees. Now all she had to do was wait.

Finally! The tight knot in Bits's stomach loosened a little. Maybe they'd make it after all. Watching Buck pick his way through the river birch, she realized how much she'd missed seeing him. Head down, he sniffed the ground. Every so often he stopped dead. Bits wondered if he was just doing it to irritate her. "Come on, move it!" she said. If only

he'd come close enough to eat out of her hand again. She moved slowly toward him, holding out half a carrot. He eyed her carefully.

"I know," she said. "Don't worry. I'm not going to yell or throw things at you." After what seemed like an eternity, he took the carrot from her fingers. "Good boy."

He finished, and looked up for more. Bits gave him a whiff of the apple, then inched her way back into the pen. "Come on." She was terrified that he wouldn't follow her, but he edged forward.

A squirrel chattered above their heads. Suddenly a pinecone plummeted to the ground right in front of Buck. He jumped and retreated back into the river birch.

"Wait! It wasn't me!"

The squirrel chattered angrily. Buck swished his tail back and forth and stared at Bits.

"See, it's a squirrel." She pointed to the noisy creature, then held out the apple and inched her way toward him. She knew he wouldn't come any closer to the pen today. It would be all she could do to keep him eating out of her hand. Whatever possessed her to try to scare him?

Buck didn't show up at all on Wednesday. Bits nearly cried with frustration as she walked home. Maybe Chris would have an idea. She'd ask tomorrow at lunch.

"Dad says that the deer are in peak rut now. I overheard him tell Larry," said Chris. She took a swallow of milk. "I don't think he likes to talk about rut with me." She grinned slyly. "Maybe he thinks I don't know about sex yet."

Bits barely listened to her friend. There were only two more days to get Buck into the pen.

That afternoon when Bits got off the bus, a black pickup with oversized tires was speeding down the road. A cloud of dust trailed behind it. Then the engine slowed, idled for a few seconds, and revved as the truck accelerated. Was this driver scouting for deer tracks, too? Bits ran toward the house.

Taking up her watch next to the bedspring, Bits covered her ears. Gunshots sounded from every direction today as hunters readied themselves for opening day.

"Please show up, please show up," Bits chanted over and over. She wrapped her arms around herself. "Please God, I'll never say I hate living up here again; just let me see Buck. I'll help Mom more, and I'll forgive Dad for bringing us here. Please God, just don't let him die because of me." Finally darkness forced her to give up. She felt tiny beneath all the trees, like a fragile sapling in a giant forest.

On Friday afternoon, Bits felt knots of determination filling her stomach. Today was the day. It had to be! She rubbed the boards and trees until the

apple scent in the air was so thick and sweet, no deer could resist it. Then she paced from one end of the pen to another. This was their last chance. Hunting season opened tomorrow. The woods would be crawling with hunters.

Had she heard something? Yes! Please, God, let it be him. A deer poked his head out between two river birch. "Thank God," she whispered. "Oh, Buck, am I happy to see you."

Buck cocked his head at her.

"Don't give me that innocent look. I haven't been able to eat or sleep for a week because of you." She picked an apple from her backpack. "Come on. I'll share this with you." Bits took a bite and held the rest out to Buck. He climbed the slope to her. His black nose quivered over her outstretched hand.

"That's right," cooed Bits. "Take the nice sweet apple."

Buck's dark upper lip tugged at the fruit.

"Good boy," praised Bits. The deer pulled again at the apple in her hand. Bits slid one foot back, then the other, slowly inching her way into the pen. Buck followed her, nipping at the apple in Bits's hand. He stretched his neck as far as he could, but Bits drew the apple back from him. He took a step into the pen. The bed spring squeaked as Buck pushed past it. He started at the foreign noise, but the lure of the apple was stronger than his fear.

"It's okay," breathed Bits. She let him have an-

other bite and pulled the apple back. "Don't be scared. We're almost there."

The sun was dipping behind the trees. Bits rolled the half-eaten apple into the pen and flattened herself against the white pine. Buck was in. Now she had to get to the bedspring before Buck finished eating. She reached across the entrance for the spring. He turned his head toward her. She stopped. "It's okay," she whispered, "just keep eating."

She heaved the bedspring off the ground with all her strength. Buck stopped eating. His tail raised in alarm. He bolted for the opening.

"No!" She couldn't let him get away! Bits threw herself and the bedspring at the white pine. The steel coils vibrated with the impact. Buck leaped to the other side of the pen, throwing himself against the boards. Bits fumbled with the rope and tied it. She'd done it! Buck was safe!

"I'll be right back." She ran to the house. "I got him!" she called. "He's in the pen."

Mom held the kitchen door open for her. "Good for you."

"I need something for water."

Mom reached into a bottom cupboard and pulled out a large roasting pan. "Will this do?"

"Perfect." Bits filled it only halfway with water, but she was still drenched by the time she reached Buck's pen. The bottom boards were high enough off the ground for Bits to slide the pan into the pen.

Buck trotted away from her. He hugged the edge of the pen, searching for a way out.

Mom had followed her down, carrying the top half of the roaster filled with corn. When Buck picked up her scent, he went wild with fear, battling the fence with his antlers and hooves.

"He knows you're here," Bits said, as she watched his frantic search for a way out.

Mom peered through the dusk into the pen. Buck snorted. "So that's your deer." She paused. "He's beautiful, Bits." She looked inside again. "But I'm scaring him, and I have to get back to Jason anyway. Don't stay out here too long."

Bits slid the pan of corn under the fence. Then she scrambled up onto the bedspring gate. The coils sang under her weight. Teetering precariously, she half jumped, half fell into the pen.

"It's okay," said Bits, raising herself from the ground. Buck's eyes looked wild. He raced the length of the pen and back, keeping as far away from her as the confined space permitted. Bits sat down next to the corn and waited for him to settle down. "Why don't you come over here and eat something?"

It was pitch black before he finally calmed down. Bits's legs were cramped from her long vigil, but she didn't dare move. At last she felt the tiny hairs of Buck's muzzle tickle her hand.

She reached up tentatively and scratched his

neck. "I'm sorry, Buck. It's for your own good, you know. It's only for sixteen days." She caressed his cheek. "But you can stay longer if you want."

The darkness surrounded them, but Bits remained with her deer until the beam of a flashlight played over the trees. "Bits! I want you in *now*." Reluctantly she stood up.

"I gotta go," she whispered.

18

Bits was jolted awake by the sound of a gun going off. Hunting season had begun. She leaped out of bed in a panic before she remembered that Buck was in his pen. He was safe. She pulled on her clothes to the awful sound of more gunshots, then pulled the curtains apart and peeked out the window. It was barely light outside.

Bits shivered. It was cold in her bedroom, but the shiver wasn't because of that. Everything was different now. For the next sixteen days, it would be dangerous around the woods—for people as well as deer. Poor Buck. He was hearing the guns, too. He was probably more scared than she was.

Dad was opening the refrigerator when Bits walked into the kitchen. He'd gotten home after she'd gone to bed last night. Did he know about Buck and the pen?

"Your mom and I had a talk last night, Bits," he said. "I know you did what you felt you had to do."

Bits let out a sigh of relief, then pulled on her jacket.

"Hold it—I have something for you." He took an orange vest out of a bag. "I bought one for each of us. I don't want any hunters thinking we're deer."

Bits slipped her arms into the holes, then tied the dangling strings. She felt like a traitor having a hunting vest on, but it did make her feel safer. You'd have to be blind not to see *this* color.

"Stay on our property," said Dad gruffly. "I don't want you wandering around out there—do you hear me?"

Bits nodded. She wasn't going to argue. It scared her just hearing all those guns.

She filled a pail of water to pour into Buck's pan. The water sloshed over the sides as she carried it down to the pen.

Chris was right. It *did* sound like the Fourth of July. Gunshots punctured the air from every direction: two here, one across the lake, four way off in the distance. Was Chris out there? Bits hoped not.

The water in the pail splashed her knees, forcing Bits to slow down. She wound through the trees. Would Buck be glad to see her?

She caught sight of one of the deer stand boards jutting out between the jack pines. Something was wrong. Dropping the bucket, she raced to the pen. She gasped. One of the boards hung twisted on its

nails. Two lay on the ground. The pen was empty. Buck was gone.

Bits picked up one of the boards from the ground. The wood was dented and split. She closed her eyes. He'd kicked the boards out. It was those damned short nails.

A gun went off across the swamp. Bits dropped the board. She had to find him!

"Buck! Buck!" she screamed, running down to the trail. "Where are you?" Where would he go?

Bits searched the clearing, but there was no sign of Buck. A gun went off across the creek. She jumped. What should she do? Running through the woods calling Buck's name like a mad woman wasn't going to help. She might even scare him right into some stupid hunter's line of fire. She'd never forgive herself if that happened. Calm down, she told herself. Think!

Bits imagined Buck walking up to a hunter, his trusting eyes searching for an apple in hands that held a gun instead. She shook the vision off. "He's hiding somewhere." Saying it out loud helped her believe it. "So if he's hiding, it'd be around here. I've got to keep hunters away." Bits bolted for the house. Mom and Dad would help.

Bits yanked the door open, her lungs burning from the cold air. She stumbled into the kitchen. "He's gone!" She wheezed.

"Oh, no, Bits," said Mom. "How?"

"He kicked . . . some of the boards . . . or pushed them with his antlers. I don't know," panted Bits. "They're going to get him. We *can't* let them get him. Help me! We've got to keep the hunters away!"

Her parents stared at her. There was pity, but no help in their eyes.

Bits turned. "Thanks—thanks a lot." The door slammed behind her. Her side ached as she ran up the driveway. She had to stop and put her hands on her knees to catch her breath.

She reached the road at last. She looked to the left: no hunters that way. On the right about a quarter of a mile down around a curve, a brown truck sat parked on the opposite side of the road.

She heard an engine behind her. Her dad's car came up the driveway. He pulled over beside her and rolled down the window.

"I have to go to work, and your mom can't leave Jason. We know how you feel about Buck, honey. And we aren't the enemy." He reached out and pulled the zipper of her coat up. "Your mom called Chris. She's going to help you with the hunters. Mom will go pick her up as soon as Jason's had his breakfast."

"Great. Buck could be dead by then."

"I love you, honey," said Dad. Then he was gone down the road toward town.

Bits saw movement down by the truck as Dad's car passed it. Three orange-clad men were lifting something onto the flatbed. The hardtop over the bed and the angle kept Bits from seeing what it was.

The three hunters climbed into the cab. Bits heard them laughing. Then the engine revved and the pickup pulled onto the road. It looked like the same truck she'd seen scouting for deer tracks last week. It slowed near one of her No Hunting signs. The driver pointed to the sign and the hunter on the passenger side jumped out and ripped it off the tree.

"Hello there," called the driver, as they pulled up to her. "You don't happen to know who put these signs up, do you?"

"I did," answered Bits.

"You know, the property on that side belongs to the paper company."

Bits lied. "I thought we owned it."

"Well, you don't. I ought to know, eh, boys?" The man chuckled. "I live two miles from here. Been hunting this area for almost thirty years."

Bits held her tongue. What could she say? She clenched her fists. Did all the hunters know about the paper company land?

"Better be careful out here, little lady," said the man. "There are going to be a lot of bullets flying around today. Be seeing you." He waved as the truck pulled past.

Bits's stomach churned. The motionless bodies of

two deer lay on the lowered tailgate. They were so close, she could count the points on the one deer's antlers—six. The other deer had no antlers; it must be a doe. Bits gulped the air. Their eyes were glazed, their sides caved in, their underbellies torn open. They had been gutted. A trail of blood dotted the road behind the departing truck.

The truck stopped, and again the hunter on the passenger side ripped down one of her signs. Bits staggered into the brush beside the drive and threw up. She leaned against an aspen with her eyes shut tight, but even so she could still see the bodies.

More shots sounded from near the creek. Bits's eyes snapped open. Were they everywhere? She imagined Buck lying on a truck bed, his bright brown eyes veiled by the gray gauze of death.

"Hey, kid," She hadn't heard the hunter who was strolling toward her now. "Yeah—you, kid."

Bits hated being called "kid," especially by some-one not much older than herself—eighteen at the most. He wasn't bad looking, but his eyes were bloodshot and he had a day's growth of beard. The barrel of his gun rested against his shoulder.

"Have you seen a spike buck cross the road?"

"S-spike?" Bits's heart raced in her chest.

The hunter gave her a funny look. "Yeah, with two little antlers about this high." He indicated the height with his fingers.

Bits's knees felt weak. He was describing Buck.

"No. Why do you want to know?" She didn't want to hear the answer, but she had to.

He scratched his chin. "Thought I might have hit him. I found some hair, but no blood." He shrugged his shoulders. "Probably just grazed him."

Bits couldn't breathe. It couldn't be Buck. It just couldn't.

Another pickup with oversized tires sped toward them. The driver slammed on the brakes. "Come on. Time to party." He tossed an unopened beer can out the open passenger window. The hunter caught it with his free hand. He grinned at Bits as he jumped into the truck.

Bits hated them—hated their guns, their pickup, their beer. "Didn't you see the signs!" she screamed. But the truck had already sped away.

Bits plunged into the woods. It wasn't Buck! She had to find him, make sure. What if it *was* Buck? The jerk had said he'd just grazed him. It would be okay.

Where would he go? Bits racked her brain. Chris had told her about wounded deer. A thicket. That was it! Wounded deer headed for cover. The swamp!

Bits cut across the tree plantation. She stumbled over the furrows separating the rows of trees. Gunshots filled the air. Bits froze. She couldn't be scared. Buck needed her. She forced herself to continue.

The swamp was big, and to Bits's frightened eyes,

it all looked the same. She'd search in sections, starting closest to the clearing. She didn't want to waste time going over ground she'd already covered.

Bits worked her way toward the creek, then back to solid ground again, up to the trail—still no sign of Buck. Maybe that was good. Maybe the jerk had only *thought* he'd hit a deer. Bits felt her hopes rise.

She left the trail near the iron pipe and bypassed the jack pines that marked Buck's pen. At least that was one place she wouldn't have to look! She tripped over a root and fell, landing by a swamp plant that looked like a giant dried-up leaf. On the broad brown leaf, a single drop of watery-looking blood glistened. Suddenly the world caved in on her. She *knew* it was Buck's blood. Bits crawled forward into the brush. There was another drop, then another and another. The drops looked almost black against the dirty snow.

"Buck?"

He raised his head, and Bits saw the confusion and pain in his big eyes.

"It's me, Bits, your friend." She edged closed.

He thrashed himself up to a standing position. Bits gasped. On his left flank was a dark hole the size of a dime. A crooked crust of dried blood ran down his slate gray coat. He staggered away from her.

"Don't go!" pleaded Bits. "I won't hurt you. I've come to take care of you." She moved closer.

He slipped and crashed to his knees. Fresh blood

spurted out of the wound. Tears stung Bits's eyes. Buck screamed. It was like nothing Bits had ever heard. "Stop it," she screamed back. She turned to run out of the thicket, but a hand caught her shoulder.

Bits screamed again as she swung around. Chris. It was Chris.

"Buck's been shot!" Bits collapsed against her friend. "Help me. Help him."

"Okay, Bits, okay."

"I have to help him. What can I do? You have to tell me what to do. . . . "

Chris disappeared into the underbrush where Buck lay.

"Bits?" Chris came back out, her mouth set. "Your deer's been gut shot. He's been hit in the stomach or intestines. He's all torn up inside. If he doesn't bleed to death, he'll die because of poisons inside him. Even if you could get a vet, there's nothing he could do." She paused. "Bits? You can't let him suffer."

Bits's lips moved, but nothing came out. Buck's scream lingered in her mind. "No! He'll be okay. He'll be all right." He had to be.

"Bits!" Chris grabbed her arms. "I'm going to call home. Stay with your deer—for God's sake keep him *here*. Can you do that?"

"I'll try." Nothing mattered but making Buck well. Chris took off like a shot.

He'd heaved himself back onto his feet. The muscles in his hindquarters were quivering. His left
back leg almost buckled. She reached out to him,
but he lurched from her. Then his forequarters
sagged, his head drooped, and, swaying slightly, he
dropped to his front knees, then lay down.

Bits inched her way toward him. "It's okay, Buck.
We're going to make you better," she said, fighting
back her tears. Strings of saliva dripped from his
muzzle. She tried to wipe his face, but he turned his
head away. She tried a second time. He didn't have
the strength to refuse.

Buck heaved a ragged breath and laid his head
down. The whites of his eyes showed and his tongue
hung out. His rib cage pumped in and out.

"I'm sorry, Buck. I didn't mean for you to be
shot. I tried to keep you safe." Tears streamed down
her cheeks. Maybe if she had known about deer
stands, or used longer nails in the boards, or not fed
Buck . . . She wiped her cheeks with her coat sleeves.
It was all her fault that he didn't have the natural
instinct to protect himself. It was all her fault. Tears
dropped from her chin onto the ground beneath
them. She had wanted a friend so badly, but it had
been selfish to tame Buck, she knew that now. She
couldn't let him suffer now because *she* didn't want
him to die. She couldn't keep on hurting him. She
couldn't be that selfish.

Buck was panting faster. Gently she lifted his

head onto her lap. She stroked his face and neck. "It won't be long now." The quivering in his hindquarters had spread to his belly and shoulder. "I'm sorry," Bits cried. "I love you, Buck."

At last, she heard voices. They were coming. "You won't have to hurt much longer," she whispered. She tried to keep her tears from falling on his face, but she couldn't help it. One fell on his cheek, and she wiped it away. Leaning over she kissed him on the bridge of the nose. "I love you," she told him again. She stroked his soft neck one last time, then slipped his head to the ground and headed back to the others.

Chris and Jeremy were picking their way toward her. "You know what to do?" Bits heard herself say, surprised at the strength of her voice.

"Yes," answered Jeremy.

"Good."

Bits stared at the shotgun in Jeremy's hands. The black metal looked cold.

"Let's go," said Chris. She touched Bits's arm. Bits led them into the brush.

Buck heard them coming and struggled to stand. It tore Bits's heart out to see him try. Slowly he raised himself. Dried blood caked his side and belly. The wound still oozed. Leaves and pine needles were matted on his stomach where he'd been lying down.

Chris looked at her brother. Jeremy was folding

and unfolding his hands around the gun. "Can you do it?"

"What?" He looked at his sister. "Oh, sure."

Bits watched Jeremy's adam's apple go up and down as he swallowed. What was he waiting for? Couldn't he see Buck was in pain?

"Are you ready?" asked Chris.

"Huh?" He glanced at the two girls, then nervously dug two shells from his pocket. He loaded them into the shotgun, licked his lips, then raised the gun so that the butt rested against the crook of his shoulder.

Buck staggered and fell again. He cried out as his wounded flank hit the ground. Bits swiped at the wetness running down her cheeks. Now. Do it now. Out of the corner of her eye, she saw Jeremy lower the gun, then quickly raise it back up again.

"Come *on*," said Chris.

Jeremy let the gun swing down against his leg. "I—I can't. Here." He pushed the gun toward Chris. "I don't care how much Dad and Larry tease me. I can't shoot anything. I just can't!" Head down, he barged through the trees behind them.

Chris looked at the shotgun and then at Bits.

Buck grunted as he tried to get up again.

"I want you to do it," said Bits.

"You'll hate me."

"No, I won't. Please," begged Bits. "It hurts."

Chris slowly raised the shotgun. She looked over at Bits. "Maybe you'd better not look."

"I have to," said Bits. It was the only thing she had left to give Buck. He was on his feet again, looking at her. Bits stretched her hand toward him.

The shot shattered the air. Buck fell.

19

Bits sat in Buck's pen tossing corn kernels, one by one, through the gaps in the boards.

"Can I join you?" Mom asked, and sat down beside her. "You know, when I was a nurse, once in a while people asked me to help them end their lives."

Mom had never talked much with her about the hospital. Bits let a handful of kernels trickle through her fingers. "So?"

"I couldn't help them, of course. But sometimes I wonder. . . ." She looked at Bits. "I think you did the right thing for Buck."

Could doing the right thing in the end ever make up for taming him in the first place? Bits didn't think so.

"I better get back," said Mom. "I have soup on the stove." She got up and brushed off her pants. "Oh, Chris called. That's some friend you've got there." She disappeared around the side of the pen.

Bits pulled a tiny box out of her pocket. Inside were the deer earrings Dad had bought for her in Duluth. Getting up, she walked to the bedspring and bent the wire of one earring over a steel coil. The sun coming through the trees glinted off the silver surface. She would leave it there forever, to remind her of Buck and their friendship.

The other earring she planned to give to Chris. She already knew what she'd say on the card. "For my best friend. Love, Bits."